GUT CHECK!

Joe glanced back over his shoulder and down the long hallway. Two guards were running toward him, their clubs drawn and ready.

"Run for it!" Joe yelled to Mike and Frank. A moment later the double doors ahead of him crashed open. Two more guards appeared, blocking their escape.

Joe scanned the hallway quickly. He noticed a group of pipes about a foot below the ceiling. He crouched slightly and put all his force into a leap upward. Wrapping his hands around the pipes, he swung forward and bent at the waist, then kicked out with both feet. His left foot connected solidly, catching one of the guards just below the ribs. The guard gave a loud grunt and fell backward.

Joe wasn't so lucky with his right foot. The other guard saw it coming, dodged to the side, and managed to land a blow on Joe's thigh with his club. Joe released the pipes. As he fell to the floor, he saw the second guard raising his club for another blow, this one aimed at his head. . . .

Available from ARCHWAY Paperbacks

TOXIC REVENGE

FRANKLIN W. DIXON

AN ARCHWAY PAPERBACK
Published by POCKET BOOKS
New York   London   Toronto   Sydney   Tokyo   Singapore

AN ARCHWAY PAPERBACK *Original*

An Archway Paperback published by
POCKET BOOKS, a division of Simon & Schuster Inc.
1230 Avenue of the Americas, New York, NY 10020

Copyright © 1994 by Simon & Schuster Inc.
Produced by Mega-Books of New York, Inc.

ISBN: 0-671-79467-1

First Archway Paperback printing January 1994

10 9 8 7 6 5 4 3 2 1

THE HARDY BOYS, AN ARCHWAY PAPERBACK and colophon are registered trademarks of Simon & Schuster Inc.

THE HARDY BOYS CASEFILES is a trademark of Simon & Schuster Inc.

Cover art by Brian Kotsky

Printed in the U.S.A.

IL 6+

Chapter

1

"Do you see Joe and Vanessa anywhere?" Callie Shaw asked her boyfriend, Frank Hardy. She stood, scanning the streams of students converging on the doors to the Bayport High School auditorium. "I told Vanessa we'd wait for them out here."

At six foot one, Frank Hardy could easily look over the heads of most of the crowd. His brother, Joe, was an inch shorter than he was, but his wavy blond hair made him easy to spot.

"There they are," Frank said, pointing to his right. "Just in time, too, if we want decent seats. I didn't think this talk would draw so many people."

"Everybody's really excited about Project Planet Earth," Callie replied. "You and Joe did your part for the environment when you solved

1

that kidnapping case in the Venezuelan rain forest. Now we all have a chance to help out here at home."

"Maybe I should nominate you for chairperson of the steering committee," Frank teased.

Joe and Vanessa arrived in time to hear this. "Great idea," Vanessa said. "How about it, Callie?"

Frank smiled. Vanessa Bender was new to Bayport High's student body, and to Joe Hardy's life. Tall and slim, with long ash-blond hair and blue-gray eyes, she was a very talented computer artist.

"No, thanks, Vanessa," Callie said with a twinkle in her eyes. "I'd rather be out talking to people about the project than sitting around a table arguing about what to do next."

"What *we* do next is easy," Joe said. "We go in and find seats—while there are still some to find."

As they entered the auditorium, Frank spotted the big frame and broad shoulders of their friend Biff Hooper. He was standing near the front, next to five or six empty seats. Biff saw them and waved, then pointed to the seats. Frank and the others joined him.

As they sat down, there was a burst of shrill feedback from the public address system. Tall, skinny Fred Margolis, the student body president, walked quickly onto the stage, grabbed one of the microphones, and covered it with his hand until the electronic wail faded.

"Okay, everybody," Fred said. "Let's get started. Bayport High's Project Planet Earth is going to be awesome. Am I right? Let's hear it!"

There were a few scattered shouts of "Yea!" and "Go, Fred!" and some polite applause.

"Bad move," Callie whispered to Frank. "He should have got the crowd worked up before he asked them to start cheering."

"Shhh!" hissed someone in the row behind.

Callie peeked over her shoulder, wrinkled her nose at the hisser, then settled back in her seat.

Fred continued, "The planning committee for Project Planet Earth has done a terrific job. I'd like to ask Alice Kim, who's been chairing it, to come up and give us an overview. Alice?"

A girl with short dark hair bounced up onto the stage. She was wearing a black T-shirt on which was printed a huge photo of earth as seen from space. Frank knew her as someone who managed to find the environmental angle to any topic that came up.

"Here's the plan, people," Alice began. "We're going to kick off the project next Friday with a big rally. We'll have a band and everything. Then everybody who wants to take part will sign up for various pro-earth activities. At the end of the month, we're going to stage a giant carnival with the theme of Save Our Planet, and invite the whole town to join us. By the time we're done Bayport should be aware of the way we're spoiling our environment and want to start doing something about it."

"What pro-earth activities will there be, exactly?" somebody called from the back of the auditorium.

Alice hesitated. "Well, different people on the planning committee had different ideas. Maybe I should let them speak for themselves." She scanned the audience. "Ah, Mike? Do you want to lead off? You all know Mike Tano."

The guy who hurried up onstage was of medium height and build, with black hair that fell down over his forehead. He was wearing khaki pants and a white button-down shirt with the sleeves rolled up above his elbows.

"Who is he?" Vanessa whispered to Callie.

"He edits the school paper," Callie replied.

"Shhh!" the same person in the row behind them hissed. Callie rolled her eyes and shrugged her shoulders.

Mike clutched the microphone with both hands and leaned close to it. "The key to a successful project is a clean-up effort for the city," he boomed. "The key to this is good communication—communication through the Bayport High School *Review*. I say we organize a raffle to raise money to upgrade the *Review*'s computer system. With better equipment, the *Review* could make communicating about Bayport's environment more efficient. That would benefit our paper, our school, our city, and ultimately our whole planet."

Frank chuckled to himself. Why had Mike stopped there? What about the solar system? The Milky Way? Even the universe? Did he honestly believe the school would buy into his plan to help the paper by pretending it was related to the environment?

"Just remember," Mike concluded. "Never underestimate the power of the press! Thank you."

As he was coming down from the stage, Chuck Franklin, the captain of the basketball team, walked up to the mike that had been set up in the center aisle.

"Alice, Fred, can I say a word?" he asked.

Alice, now back at the mike onstage, nodded.

"I noticed that this carnival you're planning comes during basketball season," Chuck said. "We've got a terrific team this year, one that'll make everybody proud to be here at Bayport High. So I'd like to move that we have a raffle at the carnival and use the money for a monster pep rally for Bayport's own basketball team."

"Chuck, what does basketball have to do with saving the planet?" Alice asked.

Chuck was silent. He obviously hadn't thought of that until that very moment.

Frank turned to Callie and muttered, "Maybe somebody could paint a basketball to look like a globe."

Vanessa overheard. "Great," she said. "And we could do a poster of Chuck, in uniform,

5

about to take a free throw with it, with the caption, It's our planet, don't throw it away!"

"Why not, Don't dribble it away," Biff suggested.

All of them cracked up. So did some of the people in the next row, who had overheard the exchange.

"Well, thanks for your suggestion, Chuck," Alice said. "We'll all keep it in mind. Is there anyone else? Yes?" She pointed to a hand on the left side of the audience.

A girl with big eyes, long dark hair, and an expensive camera slung over her shoulder hurried over to the microphone. "I'm Tiffany Alba," she said breathlessly, "and I'm vice-president of the school camera club, and I think that instead of a raffle, we ought to have a big photo exhibition about the planet, with prizes and publicity and all, and—" She stopped to take a breath, then added, "Well, that's it, really. That's my idea—a photo show. I think it'd really make people think."

As she returned to her seat, a speaker from the Outdoor Club stepped up to the mike. He urged everybody to show their commitment to the environment by joining the Outdoor Club.

"This is getting ridiculous," Callie said.

Frank couldn't help agreeing. There was a whole auditorium full of students eager to get involved in environment projects, but nobody was giving them any real ideas about what to do. It was pitiful. He looked over his shoulder and noticed that some kids were starting to drift out the door. He didn't blame them. He was starting to think seriously about leaving, too.

Callie nudged him. "Look," she whispered. "Erika Rodoski is going to speak. Because of all the work she's been doing on student council, people are already talking about her for student body president next year."

Frank watched as a girl with wavy light brown hair walked confidently across the stage toward the mike. She said a couple of words quietly to Alice, then turned and gave the audience a warm smile. The hubbub in the room quieted slowly.

"It's great to hear so many fresh ideas," she began. "This is a great moment. We're going to make Project Planet Earth an event we'll all remember—the whole *city* will remember—for years to come."

Frank sat up straighter. Something about the way Erika spoke gave him the feeling that she was the only one in the room who had a worthwhile idea, and now she was about to share it with him. He glanced down his row and saw that Callie, Vanessa, Joe, and Biff were also listening intently. Some of the students who had stood up to leave sat down again.

Erika continued in her clear, confident voice. "Now isn't the time to just throw a party for the environment or show photographs of it, or raise money to write more about it. We students of Bayport High need to show our neighbors that we can all make an important contribution every day—by recycling.

"Most people already know that recycling cans and bottles and newspapers is the law in Bayport. But lots don't do it because—let's face it—it's inconvenient and the laws can't really be enforced," Erika continued, her gaze moving gravely across the audience. "People get confused about what can be recycled and what can't, and they forget what day the recycling companies come to pick up the stuff. So they stop trying, and more and more landfills are being closed all over the world."

"So what can we do about it?" someone called from the audience.

"We can concentrate on recycling one thing—plastics," Erika answered forcefully. "Most people in the country still throw out plastics because they don't know which kinds of plastic containers can be recycled. With our help, Bayport is going to show the state and maybe even the country that there's a better way."

She paused for a moment, and Frank noticed that Alice, who had headed the planning committee for the project, looked baffled. Whatever Erika was about to propose, she had obviously kept it to herself until now.

"Most of you know the United Plastics—UniPlast—factory on the south side," Erika said. "It's one of Bayport's biggest industries. Well, as of tomorrow, there will be a new approach to recycling plastics, to be pioneered by our very own Project Planet Earth. Sol Stone, the chief executive officer of UniPlast, is a friend of my parents and a man with forward-looking ideas. He's here with us today. If it's all right with Alice, I'd like to ask him to come up onstage to tell you about his plans."

Alice, looking more baffled than before, said, "Sure, Erika."

"Thanks," Erika said. "Everybody, please welcome Mr. Sol Stone."

Frank joined the crowd in clapping as a man of about forty walked briskly from the side of the room to the stage stairs, which he took two at a time. His well-tailored suit, freshly polished shoes, and neatly combed dark hair made him fit Frank's concept of a successful businessman so exactly that it was eerie. The only feature that didn't fit was his slightly off-center nose, which gave him the appearance of someone who had boxed in college.

"Thank you all for inviting me," Stone began as the applause died down. "And special thanks to Erika Rodoski, whose wonderfully creative ideas inspired what I'm going to say today. UniPlast is behind Project Planet Earth one thousand percent. All you have to do is go door-to-door and explain to people the kinds of plastic containers that can currently be recycled. If you'll do that, we'll supply you with receptacles for the plastics and lend you UniPlast vehicles to help collect them. Most important, I am proud to announce that our company has just finished installing a state-of-the-art recycling facility that will return everything you gather to useful life. What's more, we'll pay full commercial rates for the plastics, so your school can make money while doing good."

The clapping was louder this time, and mixed with cheers. A kid who was a sophomore ran up to the floor mike and shouted, "I move we elect Erika Rodoski to head the recycling project!"

As the cheers continued to resound, Frank noticed a girl with a dark ponytail, tinted glasses, and an expression of sheer fury march up onto the stage.

"Uh-oh," Callie murmured. "Here comes trouble. Lucy Velez and Erika have been total enemies ever since Erika beat Lucy in that student council election last year."

"That's right," Frank said. "That got pretty rough, didn't it? Lots of name-calling."

"Right," Callie replied. "I hope Lucy—"

Lucy Velez dashed up to Sol Stone and grabbed the microphone from his hand. He stepped back and glanced over at Erika for an explanation.

"Don't do it, people!" Lucy shouted. "Uni-Plast is sponsoring this program to fool us into thinking the company cares about the environment, but plastics factories like this one are terrible polluters. Are we going to let UniPlast buy us out? I say no! I say we have to choose, right now. Are we on the side of the polluters or the planet?"

"Now, hold on—" Stone started to say, stepping forward.

Erika moved more quickly than he did and pulled the mike out of Lucy's hand. "That's nothing more than a cheap smear," she declared into the microphone. "UniPlast is well known for its pro-earth policies. Today's announcement is just one more example of that. You'll be able to hear it for yourselves, if certain power-mad publicity fiends will just let our guest finish what he was saying."

Lucy, red-faced, grabbed the microphone back. "She's lying to you!" she shouted at the audience. "She's just using her family friend to buy her way into the leadership of *our* project. If you let her, Project Planet Earth is as good as down the drain!"

Grim with anger, Erika stepped in front of Lucy and reached for the mike, but Lucy backed away and held it out of range. Trying to get to the mike, Erika lunged at her attacker. Lucy shouted and pushed Erika back.

"Somebody had better stop them," Callie said, getting to her feet.

Frank stood up, too. Before he could move toward the stage, though, Erika Rodoski screamed. An instant later Frank saw her fly headfirst toward the audience.

Chapter

2

"ERIKA! ARE YOU OKAY?" Fred Margolis hurried down the steps of the stage to help Erika. As Joe watched, Erika disentangled herself from the three audience members she landed on after Lucy had pushed her off the stage. Erika was flushed with anger and embarrassment, but Joe could see she wasn't seriously hurt.

"I'm okay. It was just an accident—I guess," Erika said with a glance at Lucy, who glared at her from the edge of the stage. Lucy's arm was being firmly gripped by Sol Stone, who seemed to be angry as well.

"Well, let's try not to get carried away," Fred said. He led Erika back onto the stage and picked the mike up from the floor. "Mr. Stone has made us a very interesting offer. Does anybody want to speak about it?"

As people slowly started to line up at the floor mike, Mr. Stone let go of Lucy's arm. She moved to the back of the stage, crossing her arms in defiance. "I'm glad that's over," Joe said to Vanessa. "I was starting to wonder whether this was a rally or a wrestling match."

"A rally, obviously," Vanessa replied. "At a wrestling match, Erika and Lucy would have been dressed up as gorillas or ballet dancers or something even weirder. I would have thought a famous detective like you would know that."

Joe's grin widened. "I count on you to keep me up-to-date on the weird stuff," he said, then added a heartfelt "Ouch!" as she lightly punched him on the left arm.

All of the speakers at the mike seemed to think that UniPlast's offer should be accepted gratefully. Onstage, Lucy Velez took notes, obviously becoming more and more upset. When the fourth speaker from the floor urged a vote to accept Mr. Stone's offer, Lucy crumpled up her sheet of paper, threw it on the floor, and stalked offstage. Joe noticed Erika's smile widen a little.

When the last speaker finished, Fred suggested choosing someone to chair Project Planet Earth. Several members of the audience shouted, "Erika! Erika!" Fred asked for a show of hands. Joe turned to survey the auditorium. Well over half of the kids had their hands up.

"The vote's clear," Fred declared. "Erika,

congratulations. Do you want to take over the mike?"

Erika stepped forward, accepted the microphone, and said, "I don't know what to say, except thank you. I'll do my best to live up to the confidence you have placed in me and to make our project a fabulous success. Now, here's how I think we should do it. . . ."

As she spoke, Joe found himself nodding in approval. Erika had really thought things out. Those who wanted to take part in the plastic-recycling project would form teams of up to eight members. Each team would be assigned a neighborhood, by lot. Everybody who took part would receive a limited-edition enamel pin, and the members of the three teams who collected the most recyclables would get souvenir T-shirts.

"And that's not all," Erika concluded. "I want Sol Stone to tell you this himself. Mr. Stone?"

The UniPlast executive had been standing to one side while Erika spoke. Now he came to center stage and accepted the microphone.

"We at UniPlast believe that people who work hard for their communities deserve recognition," he said to the audience. "That's why we've decided to offer a special prize to the one team that turns in the most recyclable plastic during the project. Every member of that team will get a free, all-expenses-paid ski weekend at a Vermont resort, compliments of UniPlast."

The auditorium erupted in applause and

cheers. Erika ran over and gave Sol Stone a hug. Then she turned toward the audience, beaming triumphantly. As the noise started to die down, she leaned close to the mike and said, "Alice already told you about the kickoff rally this Friday, and the concluding carnival. Let's hear it for Alice and all the members of her committee, and the fabulous planning job they've done."

As clapping broke out again, Joe leaned over to Vanessa and muttered, "What did Callie say Erika's running for—student body president?"

Vanessa's expression was droll as she said, "Oh, no—the United States Senate, at least. If I were you, I wouldn't bet against her winning!"

"Oh, one last thing," Erika said from the stage. "We expect all of you to come to the kickoff rally and to bring at least one friend. The more people we have there, the better it'll look when WBPT broadcasts a special show on Project Planet Earth. That's right—this is your big chance to be on television. So check the notices about the project on bulletin boards around school, and don't miss the rally Friday. With your help Project Planet Earth will put Bayport High in the history books!"

As they filed out of the auditorium, Joe turned to Vanessa and said, "Well, teammate, what do you say to a ski weekend in Vermont?"

"Do you have any idea how many people are asking each other that question at this very moment?" she asked, exasperated. "Still, it would be fun, wouldn't it?"

From behind them, Frank said, "Hey, let's go for it! The worst that can happen is that we don't win, but we help the environment. We could do worse. Who should we have on our team?"

Callie, Vanessa, and Biff all said, "Me!" at the same time. Then Callie added, "Let's ask Chet."

"Yeah, and Tony Prito, too," Joe contributed. "If he has the time, that is. Lately he's been putting in a lot of hours at his job at Mr. Pizza."

"Well, why don't we all meet there today after school and figure out a winning strategy?" Biff suggested. "That way, Tony can be part of it even if he *is* working."

On Friday afternoon everyone returned to the auditorium for the monster kickoff rally. The room had been decorated with garlands of green crepe paper. A gigantic cardboard cutout of the earth hung over the center of the stage.

Frank dodged around a WBPT-TV technician who was setting up a light stand and made his way to the group of seats that Vanessa and Callie had claimed. At the front of the room the school band *oompahed* a lively march, while four members of the pep squad waved pompoms. Onstage, a local rock group was setting up. More WBPT crew members and a well-dressed reporter were preparing to videotape the show. An air of excitement filled the room.

Something glamorous and important was about to happen.

The school principal opened the program by welcoming them all and assuring them that they were striking a blow for the health of the earth. Frank glanced at Callie, who was sitting between him and Vanessa. Joe was on the other side of Vanessa, and Biff, Chet, and Tony were in the row just in front of them. The whole team was together, but they hadn't come up with a name for their team. Everybody had hooted down Chet's suggestion of We Mean Green and Biff's favorite, Recycle or Die!

Vanessa, with lukewarm support from Joe and Callie, wanted to call it Team Gaia. *Gaia*, she explained, was an ancient name for the earth. Frank was willing to settle on anything at that point. How could they compete with the other teams if they couldn't agree on a name?

After the principal finished, he passed the microphone to a representative of the Bayport mayor's office, who congratulated the students for their commitment and promised that the mayor would give the project his full cooperation.

Chet turned around to mutter, "You know, if we got all the cooperation that people keep promising us, we wouldn't need the project at all. The recycling problem would have been solved a long time ago."

"I think people *will* help," Vanessa said, "once they understand the situation. But it's up to us to show them exactly how they can help."

Chet's response was lost in the crashing opening chords of a song from the rock group. After a second song, Erika Rodoski ran up onstage, took the mike, and shouted, "Project Planet Earth—that's who we are!"

Frank squinted as the bright lights of the TV crew came on. One of the WBPT camera operators moved in on the stage, while another got reaction shots from the crowd.

Erika prowled back and forth at the edge of the stage, calling out, "Are we ready? Are we committed? Are we going to make a difference in Bayport?"

After each question, the audience shouted back, "Yeah!" Each response was a little louder, and each time the members of the pep squad shook their pom-poms harder.

"All right!" Erika called. "We are set to roll! Your response has been amazing. More than thirty teams—over two hundred students—have signed up to take part in our plastic recycling effort. That's enough to cover all of Bayport and some of its nearby neighbors as well. And this is just the beginning. Every penny we make collecting recyclable plastic will be recycled, too—into our education campaign about how we can all help to deal with the dangers our planet faces."

"Thirty teams?" Callie murmured to Frank as the audience cheered louder. "The odds aren't great for that ski weekend."

"Giving up before we even start?" Frank replied.

"Tomorrow," Erika continued, "we're going to hold workshops to help you understand exactly why we're doing what we're doing, and to give us practice at answering the questions people will ask us about the project. You'll find sign-up sheets at the door when you leave. We want as many people as possible to get this training, because it'll be the best way to guarantee that Project Planet Earth will be a success. Right now I'd like to call onstage some of the people at Bayport High who are going to help move the project along."

As Erika called their names, people started coming out from the wings one by one and waving to the crowd. They seemed to include everyone on the student council, the captains of all the sports teams, and the officers of every student club Frank had ever heard of, plus a few he hadn't. Each one got cheers from fellow club members, as well as applause from the rest of the audience.

"Now let's have an especially warm welcome," Erika said, "for someone who's always been a leader at Bayport High in helping to protect the environment, Lucy Velez."

Along with the applause, Frank could hear a murmur of comments all around him. He caught Joe's gaze and raised his eyebrows. After the long-standing feud between Erika and Lucy, and their public conflict only days earlier, Lucy's appearance at Erika's kickoff rally was noteworthy.

Lucy appeared to be embarrassed and self-conscious as she stepped into the blinding TV lights. Instead of waving as everyone else had, she walked to center stage and leaned close to the mike.

"Thanks, Erika," she said, with a catch in her voice. "We can't expect to feel the same way about how this project should be carried out, but there is one thing we can all agree on. We're going to do our best to make it a real success."

Lucy was apparently the last student to be introduced. Erika stepped to one side and made a gesture that included everyone onstage, then raised her hands over her head to clap. Everyone in the auditorium joined in.

Callie turned to Frank. "Erika's done a remarkable job," she whispered. "She's managed to rope in just about everybody who counts at Bayport High."

Frank pretended to be hurt. "Oh, yeah?" he retorted. "What about us? Don't *we* count?"

When the applause died down, Erika said, "It's time to draw lots, to see what neighborhood each team will have. To help me with this, I'd like to ask Bayport High School's most famous team, our own detective duo, Frank and Joe Hardy!"

Callie burst out laughing. Frank felt his face turn red as he and Joe hurried down the aisle and climbed the steps to the stage.

20

Erika stepped into the wings and returned with a large-size coffee can with a Project Planet Earth sign taped to it and a stack of envelopes. She handed the coffee can to Joe. "These envelopes contain maps of specific neighborhoods," she explained. "And in the can are slips of paper for each of the teams. I'm going to ask Frank to draw the slips one by one, and we'll match them with an envelope. Okay?"

"Sure," Frank said.

Joe removed the plastic lid of the coffee can. Deliberately turning his head away, Frank reached into the can to select the first slip of paper. His fingers encountered something that definitely wasn't paper, something that was wet and gooey and slimy.

"Yuck!" Frank said, making a disgusted face. He jerked his hand out.

There was a sound, as if everyone in the audience drew in a breath at the same moment. Somebody near the front let out a scream. Frank saw that his hand was dripping with dark red blood.

Chapter

3

JOE STARED IN HORROR at his brother's bloody hand. "Frank, are you all right?" he asked.

"Get the school nurse!" Erika yelled.

"Calm down, everybody. I'm fine," Frank said, speaking into the mike. "I'm not really bleeding."

Joe relaxed a little, then peered inside the coffee can. There was almost an inch of some red substance at the bottom. The folded slips of paper were soaked in it. Joe pulled a handkerchief from his back pocket and handed it to his brother. "Here," he said.

"Thanks," Frank replied. He wiped off his hand, then gingerly sniffed the handkerchief. "I know what this stuff is—it's fake blood. They sell it in tubes at Halloween. Remember when Chet dressed up as a vampire?"

"What did you say was inside the can?" Erika asked Joe.

He tilted the can to let her see inside.

Erika's face went dead white. "I'll get her for this," she whispered. Then, as Joe was about to ask what she meant by that, she took a deep breath and returned to the microphone.

"Sorry, everyone," she said, in what was almost a cheerful voice. "I'm afraid the drawing will have to wait. Something was spilled all over the slips. We'll see that all of you know what your territories are. Thanks to everyone for supporting Project Planet Earth, and don't forget to sign up for tomorrow's workshops as you leave."

The applause was drowned out by the sound of conversation as the audience stood up and began to file out. The people onstage started to leave as well. The TV reporter and her crew made their way to the stage, stopping students to interview them.

"Frank? Joe? I need your help," Erika said quietly. "Someone just tried to wreck our rally with that stupid practical joke. I think I know who did it, but I want to be sure."

Frank caught Joe's eye. Joe gave a slight nod. He thought "stupid practical joke" was a good description of what had happened, but if Erika wanted them to find out who'd done it, they would do their best.

"Where was this can kept when you were onstage?" Frank asked.

Erika frowned. "I put it and the envelopes on a table just offstage. I didn't say anything about it to anyone, but whoever saw it there would have seen the sign on it and known that it had something to do with the project."

"Let's take a look," Joe suggested.

Erika led them offstage and pointed to a wooden table near the panel where the lights were operated. "That's where I left the stuff," she said.

Joe bent down and fished something out from under the table, then showed it to her and Frank. It was a white plastic tube, like a king-size toothpaste tube, with a sketch of a Dracula-like face. Vampire Blood, the label read. Plenty Scary, Perfectly Harmless. Won't Stain Clothes.

Joe touched the mouth of the tube with his index finger, then held up that finger. It looked as if he had just cut himself.

"Pretty convincing," Frank said, turning to Erika. "So now we know how, but we still don't know who. About half of the people you introduced came out from this side of the stage. Is that right?"

"I guess so," Erika replied. "But do you think somebody would have dared pour that stuff into the can with other people standing around? *I* don't."

"Were any of them back here alone?" Joe asked.

Erika hesitated, then said, "Well, yes—one of them was. The last person I introduced."

24

"Lucy Velez?" Frank frowned. "You said you thought you knew who was responsible. Was it Lucy you were talking about?"

Erika blinked, then lowered her eyes for a moment. Finally she said in a tired voice, "Listen, I really appreciate your offer to help, guys, but let's forget it, okay? Like, why make a big deal over a dumb practical joke?"

Joe motioned to Frank with his head in the direction of the exit, then said, "Sure, Erika. We'll catch you later."

As they left the auditorium, Joe said in a low voice, "Whether Erika wants to come out and say it or not, it seems like it was Lucy, doesn't it?"

"I'm not so sure," Frank replied. "How long would it take to squeeze that tube of gunk into the can—ten, fifteen seconds? The odds are, everybody backstage was too busy worrying about their entrances to notice what anyone else was up to. That means the field of suspects is still wide open."

"Well, let's hope that whoever did it is finished," Joe said. "Project Planet Earth is too important to be sunk by hare-brained stunts. I'd rather spend my time collecting plastic than chasing after some turkey with a sick sense of humor."

"This is a pretty friendly neighborhood," Callie told Frank as they approached the next house on their list. "We sure got lucky with the slip Erika drew for us."

Frank rang the doorbell and stepped back next to Callie. He could hear the TV on inside the house. Neither of them liked interrupting people so close to the dinner hour, but experience had shown it was the best time to find them home.

The man who came to the door was wearing a white shirt with the collar open and the tie pulled down. "Sorry, kids. Whatever you're selling, we don't want any," he said.

After attending Erika's grueling workshops and nearly a week of going door-to-door, Frank and Callie knew what to say by heart. Frank quickly introduced himself and Callie and showed the man their official team badges, courtesy of UniPlast. Then Callie explained the project and handed the man one of the leaflets that Erika had provided. Frank waited for Callie's cue to show him the bright green plastic recycling bin with the UniPlast logo on the side.

The man listened, then pointed to the container. "You're selling those things?" he asked.

"No, sir," Frank replied. "We're giving them out to everyone who takes part in Bayport High School's Project Planet Earth. Most of your neighbors have them already. All we're asking you to do is put your recyclable plastic items in the container and leave it at the curb on Tuesdays and Fridays. We do everything else."

The man thought for a few moments, then

26

accepted the container. "Sure, why not?" he said. "We throw the stuff away anyhow. Maybe it'll save the town a few bucks on landfill fees. We pay a lot for the right to dump our garbage, you know."

Callie smiled. "We've thought of that already. It's all in the leaflet."

Frank and Callie stopped at the sidewalk to check off the house they had just visited, then picked up another container from the Hardys' black van, and headed for the next house on the block.

Callie said, "Erika did a great job researching this project. That guy wasn't the first person to mention saving money on landfill costs."

"Erika knows her stuff," Frank agreed. "Anything that helps convince people to take part is okay with me. Well, *almost* anything. Remember that guy yesterday who signed up because the green container matched the carpet in his den and he needed a new wastebasket?"

Callie giggled, then said, "I'm starting to think there are two kinds of people in the world."

"Only two?" Frank asked, breaking in.

Callie ignored him and continued on. "Those who think they're going to have to pay us to take away their recyclable plastics, and those who think *we* ought to pay *them*. A lot of people still don't seem to get it, that we're all volunteers and so, in a way, are they."

"Whether they get it or not," Frank pointed

27

out, "I think we're off to a terrific start. So far we're getting better than four out of five households signing up. Now, if we can make sure they all put their stuff out when they're supposed to, we should really rack up the points. I wouldn't be surprised if we end up in the running for that ski trip."

"Not that that's why we're doing it," Callie said solemnly. Frank looked over, noticed the twinkle in her eye, and raised one eyebrow. Callie grinned and added, "But I won't turn it down if we *do* win."

One hour and seven houses later, Frank and Callie retrieved the van and drove back to the school parking lot to compare notes with the others on their team. When they arrived they spotted Joe, Vanessa, and Biff on the outskirts of a small crowd.

"Uh-oh," Frank murmured, as he pulled into a parking slot. "I wonder what the commotion is?"

He and Callie walked over to join the crowd that was focused on a row of bright green minivans, each with a banner on the side that read Uniplast Supports Project Planet Earth.

Frank made his way to Joe and asked, "What's up?"

"Erika's latest triumph," Joe replied. "You remember the other day, when Chet was asking how we were going to collect all the stuff people put out for recycling? Well, there's part of the answer. The Planet Earth Mini-Fleet—taa-dah!"

"Meaning what?" Frank continued.

Vanessa joined them and said, "UniPlast is donating the use of ten of these vans. Each team will be able to sign one out on a rotating basis to make collections. Neat idea, huh?"

"It's amazing," Frank replied, scratching his head, puzzled. "Erika must have been confident that her plan would be accepted. UniPlast must have had this in the works for weeks. Cars aren't like pizzas—you can't just call up the dealer and order a dozen minivans in green with extra cheese and mushrooms."

Chet joined them in time to say, "Even *I* think the idea of green pizza is gross, but maybe with extra cheese and mushrooms. Who's up for a snack?"

"Maybe they already had the vans and just added the banners," Biff suggested.

"But in that case," Joe said, "why green?"

"Why not?" Vanessa said. "Lots of people suspect big industries of causing pollution. You heard Lucy at the meeting last week. So if you're buying a fleet of cars or vans, why not get them in green so everyone sees you're pro-environment? The color doesn't cost a penny more than blue or white, and it improves your public image."

"Well, let's try improving our own image by working on our strategy for the rest of the recycling drive," Frank said. "The other teams might be stiffer competition than we think." He led the group to an empty corner of the parking lot and continued, "How are we doing so far? Any comments or suggestions?"

"We're getting a good response," Vanessa said. "Almost *too* good. Joe and I had to quit early this afternoon because we gave out our last container."

"Yeah, Biff and I are running low, too," Chet said. "That must mean we're on the right track. Though we won't really know how well we're doing until tomorrow, when we make our first collection."

"Do you think we ought to go around and remind people that tomorrow is collection day?" Biff asked.

"I don't think so," Frank said. "We don't want people to feel bugged. We want them to feel good about doing their bit. But maybe we should keep track of those who *don't* put their containers out and give them some kind of gentle reminder before next Tuesday."

"I've got an idea," Vanessa announced. "How about if I print up schedules of our collection days as a reminder to everyone?"

"Great!" Joe said, beaming at her. "We should get right on that."

After some more talk about their plans for the next day, the group started to break up. Joe turned to Frank and said, "Vanessa's giving me a ride, so you can have the van."

"Okay," Frank replied. "Hey, why don't I drive by the UniPlast factory and pick up some more containers? That way, we'll be all set tomorrow."

"I'm going to hitch a ride with Vanessa, too. I've got a paper due tomorrow," Callie said. "Try to get a lot of containers."

The drive to the UniPlast plant took less than fifteen minutes. At the gate Frank explained why he was there, and the guard directed him around the side to the loading dock of the recycling facility. Frank parked the van and vaulted up onto the loading platform of the large aluminum building. There was nobody in sight, but the floor was vibrating from distant machinery.

"Hello?" Frank called. There was no response. Was he supposed to take the containers by himself? If so, he would have to find them first. He strolled through wide sliding doors into what seemed to be the facility's receiving area. The only containers in the large, windowless room were half a dozen big metal drums stacked on wooden pallets.

Frank wandered over to the drums and idly read the label on one. Apparently it contained polystyrene pellets—otherwise known as packing peanuts—used for cushioning breakable objects. Frank guessed this must be one of the products the recycling center manufactured.

Frank was wondering if he should go find someone to help him, when he heard a faint noise behind him. He started to spin around. "Hello?" he cried.

Frank didn't get to finish his sentence. A large, rough hand grabbed him around the neck, and his right arm was jerked up behind his back in a hammerlock.

Chapter

4

"LET GO!" Frank shouted as he threw all his weight back against his attacker. There was a grunt of pain as the top of Frank's head struck the other person's face. The grip on his arm loosened.

The instant his arm was free, Frank twisted around and grabbed the head of his assailant. He was starting to tighten his grip when he realized that the other man, who had short blond hair and a square face, was wearing a guard's uniform.

"What's going on here?" someone yelled. A stocky man in a hard hat and light blue overalls came running up. The name badge over his left pocket read Andersen. "I'm the foreman here. Who are you, kid, and what are you doing here?"

Frank released the guard and stepped back, but stayed alert for another attack. "I came by to pick up containers for the high school recycling project," he explained. "This guy jumped me from behind without warning. Why, I don't know."

Andersen turned to the guard and asked, "Is that how it happened, Krieger?"

The guard was rubbing his left cheek, which was red from the impact with Frank's head. He glared and said, "Well, yeah, sort of. This guy was nosing around, so I grabbed him. I got my orders about intruders."

"Listen, Krieger," Andersen said in an impatient voice. "The next time you notice somebody you're not sure about, go up and ask them who they are. Then if you're not satisfied with their answer, you ask them to leave the plant. But no rough stuff unless there's no other way to handle the situation. Is that clear? Now, apologize and go about your business."

"You may be the foreman, but you're not *my* boss," Krieger muttered, giving Andersen a sullen look.

A new voice said, "What's the problem here?"

Frank instantly recognized Sol Stone, the UniPlast president. Andersen explained what had happened and Stone's expression was grim as he turned to Frank.

"Please accept my apologies," he said. "I'm afraid we need to keep security tight here at the plant to protect some important new advances that our competitors would love to have. But that doesn't excuse this sort of behavior. Don't worry, I'll see to it that it doesn't happen again."

He focused his full attention on the abashed guard and added, "The students from Bayport High School are our guests, Krieger. I expect them to be treated with respect. Is that clear?"

"Yes, Mr. Stone," Krieger quickly said.

"Good. Andersen, would you take our young friend and show him where to find the recycling containers?"

The foreman led Frank to a storage area near the loading dock and helped him carry two stacks of containers to the van. Frank thanked him and climbed in. As he started to drive away, he glanced in his rearview mirror. Sol Stone had his hand on Krieger's shoulder and was talking to him in what seemed to be a confidential way. Andersen was standing a few feet away from the other two, obviously frustrated. Frank was impressed that the company president was so involved with his employees, but he couldn't help wishing that Sol Stone had shown up before Krieger did, not after.

"I don't get it," Vanessa said unhappily. She and Joe were standing on the sidewalk next to the Hardys' van. "Every container on this block is empty. Why did people bother to put them out if they didn't have anything for us to collect?"

"There's something funny about this," Joe replied. He and Vanessa had been making their rounds after school, and the back of the van was more than half full. They'd been having a good time, laughing and kidding around, until they came across the empty containers.

"You know what I think?" Joe continued. "I think some of our competitors have been poaching on our territory."

"Unbelievable!" Vanessa said. "Some people will do anything for a free ski vacation."

Just up the block, a white-haired man in slacks and a sweater, with a newspaper folded under his arm, picked up one of the containers and started to carry it back toward his house.

"Let's ask him," Joe suggested. He walked quickly in the man's direction and called out, "Excuse me, sir."

The elderly man turned and waited. "Yes? Can I help you?" he asked.

Vanessa introduced herself and Joe.

"Pleased to meet you," the man said. "My name's Orrin Stamp. Is there something I can do for you?"

"We're part of Project Planet Earth, Mr. Stamp," Vanessa replied. "One of our team members gave you that container for recyclable plastic, and today is collection day."

"You're a little too late," Mr. Stamp said with a chuckle. He tilted the container he was holding to show that it was empty. "One of your teammates beat you to it, about fifteen minutes ago. Too bad your project is being called off. I thought it made good sense."

"Called off?" Joe asked. "What do you mean?"

"Why, the girl who came by gave me a notice," he replied. "It said the recycling project is over after today. Here, I'll show you."

He reached into his jacket pocket to hand them a paper. Joe unfolded it and showed it to Vanessa. At the top was the Project Planet Earth logo, a globe supported by a pair of helping hands, and the Bayport city seal was next to it. It looked identical to the project's official stationery that Erika had printed the leaflets on earlier. As Mr. Stamp had told them, the flyer announced that the recycling effort was being suspended indefinitely for technical reasons.

Joe exchanged a glance with Vanessa, then asked, "Do you mind if I keep this, sir?"

"Not at all," Mr. Stamp said. "Why? Is something wrong?"

"I think this announcement is fake," Joe told him. "As of a couple of hours ago, the recycling project was still on, but somebody seems to be trying to wreck it."

"Who would do a thing like that?" Mr. Stamp asked. "And why?"

"Two good questions," Joe replied. "I think we'd better see if we can find some good answers to them. This girl who gave you the leaflet—what did she look like?"

The elderly man scratched his head. "Well, she had long dark hair, pulled back in a ponytail. I can't tell you what color her eyes were because she was wearing dark glasses."

"What about her clothes?" Vanessa asked.

Mr. Stamp frowned. "I didn't take much notice, to tell you the truth," he said. "Jeans and a down jacket, I think. Nothing odd."

"How about her car?" Joe pursued. "Did you notice that?"

"Oh, sure," he replied with a smile. "It would have been hard not to. It was a bright green minivan with the name of your outfit on a banner on the side. I remember thinking what a shame the project was being called off after someone went to the trouble of making that nice banner."

Joe caught Vanessa's eye and motioned with his head toward his own van, then said, "Thanks, Mr. Stamp. You've been a great help. And remember—the project is still on. We'll be around on Tuesday to make another collection."

On the way back to the van, Vanessa turned to Joe and said, "That description he gave us sounded like Lucy Velez. What nerve!"

"Uh-huh," Joe replied. "The trouble is, that description could cover about half the girls at Bayport High, too."

"Okay, that's true. But who besides Lucy has a reason to torpedo our campaign?" Vanessa retorted. "I bet she'd do anything to get back at Erika. She acted too easily convinced to help Erika."

"That reminds me—we'd better tell Erika about this right away. Who knows how many people think the project is off. We'll probably have to go door-to-door again," Joe said. "But there's something I want to do first." He got behind the wheel and started the engine.

"Let me guess—we're off to find the mysterious woman in dark glasses," Vanessa said.

"Right again, as usual," Joe said. "If we're lucky, she might still be riding around in our territory."

Joe slowed to let an approaching car go past, then turned left onto the next street. Ranch-style houses lined both sides of it. "This is the last section of our route, and the containers are still full."

They drove along slowly, peering up and down each cross street. Suddenly, as they were crossing Winston Lane, Vanessa said, "Wait, Joe. I see something white fastened to all those containers, starting about halfway down the block. Let's check them out."

"Are you thinking what I'm thinking?" Joe asked. He backed up and turned onto the side street. The containers in front of the first three or four houses all had a few plastic items in them. The next container, on the opposite side of the street, was empty. Vanessa was right—a piece of paper was taped to the rim of the container and to the others farther down the block.

Joe pulled the van over to the curb and parked. "Come on," he said, swinging the door open.

He crossed the street, with Vanessa right behind him. They went onto the sidewalk and bent down to peek at the paper.

"It's the same as the one Mr. Stamp gave us," Vanessa announced. "That means Lucy's already been by here."

"We don't know it was Lucy," Joe reminded her. "I'm starting to wonder if there isn't more to this than simple sabotage. Somebody is going to a lot of trouble. Also, I wonder why she stopped here, in the middle of the block?"

"Maybe she didn't have room for any more stuff," Vanessa suggested. "Or maybe she ran out of leaflets and decided to quit for the day."

"Or went home to get more," Joe added. He took the leaflet off the container and stuffed it in his jacket pocket. "As long as we're here, we should remove these notices and sabotage her sabotage."

As he straightened up, Joe glanced over his shoulder. A green minivan was coming up the block toward them.

"Look," he said. "I bet that's her now."

Vanessa turned. "Joe!" she said urgently. "She's going awfully fast. Do you think—"

Vanessa was right. The van was going much

too fast on a residential street, and it was beginning to weave from side to side. When it was
less than a hundred feet away, it abruptly
swerved up onto the sidewalk. Joe saw with horror that he and Vanessa were directly in its
path.

Chapter

5

"MOVE!" Joe shouted.

Vanessa stared, openmouthed, at the speeding van. Joe realized that she was too shocked by the sudden danger to be able to avoid it. This was no time for politeness. With one arm he grabbed her around the waist and lifted her off her feet, then boosted her a dozen feet up into the yard. Off balance, he stumbled to his knees and rolled over to join Vanessa.

The green van careened toward them, two wheels on the sidewalk, two on the street, bouncing and swaying from side to side. As the van drew level with them, its bumper caught the light plastic container and sent it sailing to treetop height. It crashed back down in the middle of the street. The van swerved back onto the street and hit the container a second time. It was crushed flat. The van then made a tire-squealing right turn and disappeared.

Joe stood up, brushed off the knees of his pants, and offered Vanessa a hand. "Are you okay?" he asked, as he pulled her to her feet.

"I think so," Vanessa said. "A little winded, that's all. It's good I had on a heavy jacket for padding. We did nearly get hit, didn't we?"

"Yeah, more or less," Joe replied.

"I guess you're used to this kind of thing," she continued, "but I'm not. I can't believe I nearly got killed. You saved my life, Joe. Thank you."

She moved closer and kissed him lightly on the cheek. Joe gave her a pleased smile, then said, "I wish I knew who that driver was. You didn't get a look at her, did you?"

"I wish I had," Vanessa said angrily. "I'd file a report in five seconds. People like that shouldn't be allowed to have licenses—"

Vanessa stopped all at once, giving Joe a dubious look. " 'Her'?" she repeated. "Why did you say 'her'? Wait a minute—of course! That was a Planet Earth van, wasn't it? And whoever was behind the wheel is the one who's been lifting our stuff and leaving those leaflets. That means she was *trying* to hit us, or at least give us the scare of our lives. I'm right, aren't I?"

"I can't be sure, but it seems that way," Joe admitted. "Either that, or she was so rattled to see us here that she lost control of the van."

"Are you sure you didn't see her?" Vanessa asked. "Was it Lucy Velez?"

Joe mentally reran those few seconds. He had looked straight at the van as it came barreling toward them, but the shifting reflections of sun and shadow on the windshield had blurred his glimpse of the driver. All he retained was an impression of dark glasses and dark hair.

"It could have been," he said cautiously. "My impression is that she matched the description Mr. Stamp gave us. But it could have been lots of other people, too."

Vanessa frowned. "What about the license plate? Those vans may look alike, but they can't all have the same license number."

Joe shook his head. "It was too muddy to make out, which is suspicious right there. The ground's too frozen to throw up mud. Come on, let's finish talking to the people who got those leaflets and go back to school. I want to find out if Lucy checked out one of the vans. Then we can see if its license plate has mud on it."

As they crossed the street, Joe picked up the flattened recycling container. The grim thought came to him that if he had reacted just a little more slowly, the speeding van might have crushed him and Vanessa instead of a plastic bin.

"The next thing we knew, that van was heading straight at us," Vanessa said to the crowded table. "I couldn't move; I was too shocked. If it hadn't been for Joe—" She fell silent but gave him a look that spoke.

It was just after noon on Saturday, and Mr. Pizza was packed with kids from Bayport High.

There was a silence as the other members of the team around the table took in what Vanessa had just recounted. Then Biff asked, "What about the van? Did you track it down?"

Joe put down his pizza slice—Sicilian, with pepperoni—and shook his head. "Nope. All of the project vans were out yesterday afternoon, and yes, Lucy Velez had one of them. But there's no particular reason to think hers was the one that tried to run us down. Or at least, we have no evidence it was hers. They all came back with clean license plates. Frank and I checked them out last night in the school parking lot."

Tony Prito, wearing his Mr. Pizza apron, leaned forward and said, "I have to get back to work, but before I do, answer me this. I don't get the leaflets. Stealing another team's plastic is really low, but you can see why somebody might do it to win the prize. But why wreck the whole project?"

"I can think of two possibilities," Frank replied. "Maybe the real point is to undermine the project, and the stealing is incidental. Somebody went to a lot of trouble getting hold of genuine Project Planet Earth stationery and printing that phony message."

45

"Undermining the project is one possibility," Chet said. "What's the other?"

Frank shrugged his shoulders. "Erika is checking with the other teams to see if any more leaflets were delivered. *If* the saboteur hits other teams besides ours, maybe the point isn't to wreck the project as a whole, but to ruin other teams' chances to win."

Joe nudged Frank and motioned with his chin toward the entrance. Lucy Velez had just walked in. She was wearing jeans, a purple T-shirt, and a black leather jacket. She stopped just inside the doorway and took off her sunglasses to scan the place. She seemed to be disappointed by what she saw or didn't see. Whoever she was expecting apparently wasn't there.

"Let's ask her a few questions," Frank murmured to Joe. They stood up and edged through the crowded room to the entrance.

"Hi, Lucy," Joe said. "You know my brother, Frank, don't you?"

"Sure," Lucy replied. "What's happening?"

"Some weird stuff," Frank answered. "Have you heard anything about Project Planet Earth being suspended because of some kind of technical problems?"

Lucy blinked in surprise. "No. When did this happen?" she demanded.

"It didn't," Joe said. "I'd better explain." He told her about the empty containers and fake leaflets he and Vanessa had found the day before, then showed her one of the leaflets.

46

"Huh," Lucy said, studying the sheet of paper. "It looks real, but if it is, this is the first I've heard of it. How about the people who're working in the project office? Do they know anything about this?"

Frank shook his head. "Nope. It's definitely a hoax," he told her. "The question is, why?"

Lucy didn't move, but Frank had the impression of a turtle withdrawing into its shell. "I think I'm beginning to see where you guys are coming from," she said warily. "And I can't say I like it one bit."

"You checked out one of the project vans yesterday after school, didn't you?" Joe asked.

"The way you ask the question, you've already looked at the records," Lucy said stonily. "Why ask me?"

"Where were you at about five-fifteen?" Joe pursued.

"None of your business," Lucy snapped. Then she seemed to reconsider. "I was driving around my team's territory and emptying containers."

"Was anybody with you?" Frank asked.

Lucy's face reddened. "Listen, what is this?" she demanded.

"A Project Planet Earth van almost ran over me and Vanessa Bender at around five-fifteen yesterday afternoon," Joe told her. "The driver had a dark ponytail and was wearing sunglasses."

Eyes narrowed, Lucy asked, "Did Erika put you up to this? Of course she did. That rat'll do anything to get what she wants, won't she? But

47

I guarantee she'll be sorry that she decided to tangle with me. I'm not planning to roll over and play dead for her, and you can tell her I said so!"

Before either Frank or Joe could react to this outburst, Lucy spun on her heel and stomped out of Mr. Pizza.

"You guys sure have a magic touch," Biff teased when they returned to the table. "You go over to talk to somebody, and two minutes later, poof! she disappears."

Mike Tano, the editor of the school newspaper, was walking by at that moment. He stopped and asked, "Somebody disappeared? Who?"

"Nobody. It was just a joke," Biff assured him. "Always on the lookout for a story, huh, Mike?"

"No real reporter passes up a lead," Mike told him.

"Hey, Mike," Joe said. "Here's something you might be interested in." He showed the newspaper editor one of the fake leaflets. "We found this on our route yesterday. Somebody is deliberately trying to undermine our recycling campaign."

"Hmm," Mike replied. "Yeah, that's interesting, Joe. Thanks for bringing it to my attention."

"What are you going to do now?" Vanessa asked.

"What, about this?" Mike said, gesturing vaguely toward the leaflet in Joe's hand. "Well,

48

I'll certainly keep it in mind. And maybe I'll find the time to follow up on it next week or the week after. I've got a lot on my plate just now."

"Next week or the week after?" Frank repeated. "By then, there may not be any story."

"Yeah, that happens," Mike said. "But listen, thanks anyway for the tip. Excuse me, there's somebody I've got to talk to."

He moved to the next table and sat down across from B. J. Russo, Bayport High's leading computer expert. B.J., who was medium height with shaggy blond hair, didn't fit the usual image of a hacker nerd. The only tip-off was his T-shirt, which showed a German shepherd sitting at a computer console, with the legend My byte is worse than my bark.

"Huh!" Callie sniffed. "Some newshound Mike turned out to be."

"I guess a hoax like this isn't really what he calls news," Joe remarked. "Maybe he hears about them all the time."

"We didn't tell him about somebody almost running us over," Vanessa pointed out.

"Reckless teenage drivers?" Chet said. "Sorry, Vanessa. He did that story two years ago."

While the others kidded around, Frank was catching snatches of the conversation behind him. From such technobabble as "Sixty-four K flash cache" and "Ten megs on the motherboard," Frank gathered that Mike and B.J. were talking about a computer. This guess was confirmed when B.J. said, "No question, Mike. This new system of yours has the capability to handle anything you're likely to throw at it. When did they say it'll come in?"

"The first part of next week," Mike replied. "I can hardly wait. The best thing to do with that piece of junk I've been writing on is use it as a boat anchor. It's about as swift as a sharpened turkey quill."

Later, as Frank and Joe were walking out to the van, Frank said, "You remember Mike telling us at that first meeting how badly the school paper needed a new computer? It sounds as if he's getting one."

"That's great," Joe said. "But I wonder where he found the money. He didn't get it from Erika, that's for sure."

On Monday afternoon Frank, Joe, and Vanessa were their team's delegates at a special meeting to discuss the results of Project Planet Earth's first week. The student council office was too small to hold everybody, so Erika moved the meeting to a classroom down the hall. After some general remarks about how wonderfully everyone was doing and about the phony leaflets, Erika started to read off the number of pounds of recyclable plastic each team had turned in so far.

When she announced Team Gaia's results, Vanessa gave Joe a grin and a quick hug. They were in the lead, with over four hundred pounds to their credit. Before Erika announced the amounts of the Green Raiders, Lucy Velez's team, she paused, then raised her voice to say, "The clear leaders so far, with six hundred forty-two pounds. Let's all give them a big hand."

As the applause swelled, Joe checked Frank and saw that he was wondering the same thing. Was Lucy's team ahead because they had been filching from other teams? This called for a much closer look.

"We've been so busy giving workshops that we haven't been able to set up a bank account for Project Planet Earth," Erika continued, "but for this first week, Sol Stone insisted on giving us the proceeds in cash. He thought it would be a good way to keep us motivated. Over ten thousand pounds of plastic that would have clogged our landfills will be recycled, thanks to our efforts. We can do better, and we will, but it's a terrific start. At eight cents a pound, that comes to more than eight hundred dollars to use in our educational campaigns, and it's all right here."

She held up a gray metal cash box, pushed the button on the catch, and the lid fell back.

Erika's face went white. "Oh, no!" she gasped. She reached in and pulled out a thick wad of folded-up newspaper. "It's gone," she cried. "Somebody's stolen our money!"

Chapter

6

FRANK JUMPED OUT of his seat and hurried up to the front of the room. He was the first to reach Erika's side. "You'd better end the meeting," he told her quickly in a low voice.

Erika blinked several times. "Yes. Yes, of course. Thanks," she said.

The project members were talking excitedly among themselves. Erika raised her hands in an attempt to quiet them down. "Let's not panic," she said. "I guess somebody likes practical jokes. All I can say is, that person has a weird sense of humor. First the leaflets and now this. That's it for this afternoon. Don't forget—go back to your teams and tell them to get out there and spread the word that Project Planet Earth is still on and off to a terrific start."

As the others reluctantly filed out, Joe joined

Frank and Erika at the front of the room. "This is no practical joke," he declared.

Erika bit her lower lip. "I'm afraid you're right," she said. "I can't believe it. The money was in this box, and now it's not. A whole week's effort by everybody in the project, gone just like that."

"How long did you have the money with you?" Frank asked.

"I went over to the UniPlast office just before lunch to pick it up," Erika replied. "Mr. Stone seemed pretty excited about giving us the cash, and I thought it was a good idea."

"So you picked up the money and put it in this cash box, then brought it back to school," Joe said. "What next?"

She hesitated again. "Well—I didn't feel like taking it to lunch with me, so I locked it in the drawer of my desk in the student government office. Unless somebody's in there, the office is kept locked, so I figured it was safe there. It seems I was wrong."

"And when did you get it from the desk drawer?" Frank asked.

"Why—right after three, just before our meeting."

"Did you look inside?" Joe asked.

"I wish I had!" Erika burst out. "I wouldn't have made such a fool of myself just now, bragging about our successes, then holding up a crummy old newspaper!"

THE HARDY BOYS CASEFILES

"Yes, let's have a look at that newspaper," Frank said. "Joe, can I borrow your pen?"

Frank took Joe's ballpoint and left the cap on, then drew a pencil from his own shirt pocket. Holding it by the pointed end, he used it and the pen to lift the folded paper.

"You think there are fingerprints?" Erika asked.

"Probably not," Frank said, with a laugh. "Bad guys have watched too many crime shows and read too many detective stories to go around leaving fingerprints. Still, people do get careless."

"Well, I know you'll find *my* fingerprints," Erika continued. "Because I picked it up just now."

"I'll keep that in mind," Frank said. "Uh-huh, just as I thought. It's a copy of the *Review,* the issue that came out today."

"Not that that's much help," Joe pointed out. "The school is full of them."

"That's true," Frank replied. "But the delivery truck from the printer got here late. I tried to get a copy at about two-thirty, and there weren't any. While I was looking, I saw the guy arrive with them."

Frank dropped the paper back into the metal box. "So the substitution must have been made after two-thirty, and before—when did you retrieve the box, Erika?"

"I can't be exact," she said nervously. "But it was a little after three. And I came straight

54

here with it. It wasn't out of my hands the whole time."

Frank recalled that this wasn't strictly true—the box had been on the table in front of Erika until she picked it up and opened it. But it *had* been in plain sight. Unless the thief was both invisible and had the knack of reaching inside a steel box without opening it, the substitution must have taken place before Erika came to the meeting, Frank reasoned.

"Eight hundred dollars is a lot of money," Joe pointed out. "We'd better call the police and report the theft."

"Oh, no!" Erika wailed. "No police! The bad publicity would ruin the project. Besides, maybe it really *was* a practical joke, and the money will be returned. I couldn't bear to get someone in serious trouble just because of a stupid joke. I'd rather just keep it to ourselves."

"You can't keep this a secret," Joe said. "Everyone who was at the meeting knows the money is missing. By this time tomorrow, everyone will know."

"Yes, but—" Erika broke off and bit her lip again. Then she said, "Joe? Frank? You'll investigate, won't you? Once you solve the mystery, we can tell the police, if we need to. But it won't be the same kind of scandal then. Please? As a favor to everyone in Project Planet Earth?"

Frank checked with Joe, who gave a slight nod. "Of course we will," he said. "We'd better get on it before everybody goes home for the day."

"For two days," Joe reminded him. "Tomorrow's a holiday—Founders' Day, remember?"

"What are you going to do now?" Erika asked.

Frank thought for a minute. "I'd like to find out who was in the student government offices this afternoon and take a look at the desk where you left the cash box," he replied.

"Sure, I'll meet you there in five minutes," Erika said. "I've got an errand to run first."

"After that, I think we should drop by the *Review* office," Frank continued. "There's a slim chance that staff members get a few copies of each issue before the rest of them are delivered."

"You think Mike—" Joe began. Frank gave him a quick warning glance. He coughed, then added, "Sorry. I was thinking of something else."

Before leaving, Frank took the cash box carefully by the corners and put it in Joe's backpack. In spite of what he had just told Erika, it was possible that the thief had left prints on the folded newspaper or box. He and Joe could check it out that evening. They had fingerprinting equipment at home.

As they walked down the corridor toward the student government offices, Joe said, "First the sabotage, then that van that nearly hit me and

Vanessa, and now this. Do you have the feeling that the situation is getting worse, fast?"

Frank nodded somberly. "On the face of it, it's a school problem, but I can't shake the feeling there's something more and bigger involved."

Erika was waiting at the student government office with a dark-haired guy in a red- and white-striped polo shirt. Frank recognized him as Miguel Santiago, one of the junior class officers.

"Listen to this," Erika said excitedly. "Miguel was in here when I put the cash box in my desk, and he stayed on for an hour or so afterward."

"Is that so?' Joe replied. "Why?"

"I was studying," Miguel said. "It's pretty quiet in here. It's a good place to hit the books."

Frank glanced at the table next to Miguel's chair. A sword-and-sorcery science-fiction novel was lying facedown, half-hidden by a spiral notebook. It wasn't the kind of reading encouraged in study hall. Miguel noticed where Frank was focused and casually shoved the novel a little farther under the notebook.

"Did anybody come in while you were here?" Frank asked, smiling to himself.

"I already told Erika. A couple of people came in, but no one went anywhere near her desk," Miguel replied, pointing to one in the corner. "And I know I locked the door when I left. When I came back about half an hour ago, it was still locked."

Frank exchanged a glance with Joe. If Miguel

could be believed—and there didn't seem to be any good reason *not* to believe him—the time frame was narrowing rapidly.

"How many people have keys for the office?" Frank asked.

Erika gave Miguel a questioning look. "Well, lots," she said. "I don't know, exactly."

"There's a key list here somewhere," Miguel said, crossing to a file cabinet and tugging open the second drawer. "Yeah, here we go."

Frank took the list and scanned the twenty or so names. Both Lucy Velez and Mike Tano were on it. He passed it to Joe, who began copying it, and went over to Erika's desk. It was pretty old and battered, but he didn't see any sign that the lock had been forced.

"Do you have the only key to the desk?" he asked Erika.

"As far as I know," Erika replied. "It hasn't been in here very long. It used to be down in the *Review* office."

Frank's eyes met Joe's. What were the odds that Mike had held on to a key to the desk? "Let's go see if Mike is still around," Frank told Joe. "Erika, we'll be in touch."

The *Review* office was just down the hall. As Frank and Joe approached, they saw that the door was slightly ajar. Frank tapped on it, then pushed it open. A group of kids were silently gathered around some layouts spread on a long table. A round-faced guy with glasses was busy entering text into an old computer to the right of the door.

"Is Mike Tano around?" Frank asked him.

"Mike? I think he went home early," the guy replied.

Frank asked if he could leave a message, and the reporter scrounged around for a pen, but couldn't find one. Then he checked Mike's desk in the corner and found a pen in the last drawer.

Just then Erika walked in with a manila envelope in her hand. "Hi, again," she said to Frank and Joe. "Did you find Mike? I want to give him some figures on our first week's results. I'll just leave them on his desk."

She went over to it. The guy gave Frank and Joe an exasperated look. "Listen, is your message urgent?" he asked. "I could try to call him. We have to lock up here in a few minutes, though."

"That's okay," Joe assured him. "We'll drop by his house on our way home. Thanks, anyway."

As they reached the school parking lot, a cold rain began to fall. It was already turning dark. Mike lived on the west side of Bayport, past the train station. As they drove along, Frank and Joe discussed the theft. Joe suspected it was part of the same sabotage campaign as the fake leaflets. Frank wasn't so sure. Couldn't it be a simple case of somebody seeing a chance for some easy, untraceable money?

They were approaching an old wooden bridge over the railroad tracks when Joe, who was driving, suddenly stiffened. "Frank," he said in a taut voice. "We've got a bright green minivan on our tail. It's pulling out to pass us. Check out the driver, will you?"

The green van accelerated and drew up level with them. Frank leaned forward and peered across Joe. As the other vehicle pulled ahead, he caught a quick glimpse of a dark ponytail and big sunglasses.

"Hold on!" Joe shouted. The green van suddenly swerved to the right, directly into the path of the Hardys' van. Joe twisted the wheel and slammed on the brakes. The rear end fishtailed on the slippery boards, and the van began to slide to the right, toward the edge of the bridge. Only a dilapidated wooden guardrail stood between Frank and Joe and a thirty-foot fall to the railroad tracks below.

Chapter

7

THE INSTANT JOE FELT the van start to skid, he cranked the steering wheel all the way to the right. He began to pump the brakes, holding them down for a fraction of a second, then releasing them for a fraction of a second before pressing down again.

As suddenly as the van had started its sideways trip, it straightened out. At the same time it slowed enough for Joe to get back some measure of control. He steered carefully away from the rail and brought the van to a halt.

"Whew!" he said.

"I'll double that," Frank replied, gazing out his window at the drop to the tracks.

Joe stared ahead. "There's not much point in trying to catch that van," he said. "It could be almost anywhere by now. Did you get a look at the driver?"

"Not really," Frank admitted. "How about you?"

"I was keeping my eyes on the road and my mind on my driving," Joe said.

"It's a good thing, too," Frank replied. "As for the driver, she reminded me of Lucy Velez, but all I really saw was a ponytail and sunglasses. Oh—and a muddy rear license plate."

Joe gave a grim smile. "That has a familiar ring to it," he said. "What gets me is that she must have followed us all the way from school without my noticing. I must be slipping."

"Let's not talk about slipping after what just happened," Frank suggested. "And maybe she didn't follow us. Maybe she just happened to see us go by, recognized us, and decided to take a shot. We don't even know that she meant for us to go off the bridge. She might have simply wanted to give us a scare."

"She did that," Joe said. He checked his mirror, then pulled back out onto the bridge and continued toward Mike's.

Mike Tano's house was one of half a dozen on a dead-end street with a little loop at the end. Behind the houses was a densely wooded area. "That's the Water District reservation," Frank said. "It's really quiet around here."

When they got out of the van, Joe paused for a moment, then cracked, "Quiet? Listen to that owl hooting."

They rang the doorbell and waited while the porch light went on. They introduced themselves to the woman who opened the door.

"Frank and Joe Hardy?" she repeated, swinging the door wider. "Come in. I've heard so much about you two. Mike's a great admirer of your detective skills. Go on up. His new computer just came today, and he's busy trying it out. His room's on the left at the head of the stairs."

Joe led the way. The door to Mike's room stood open. A powerful computer system was sitting on the desk near the window. On the floor was a stack of cartons emblazoned with the name of a leading mail-order computer company.

"Mike?" Joe called, from just inside the door. The room was empty and silent.

"He must be around somewhere," Frank said. He crossed the room and studied the mailing label on one of the cartons. "Interesting," he continued. "The order for this gear apparently went in a couple of weeks ago. And look—the computer's power light is on."

Frank leaned over and touched one of the keys, then jumped back as the computer let out a series of loud quacks.

"What did you do?" Joe demanded, hurrying to Frank's side. The quacking sound continued.

"Nothing," Frank said. Suddenly the monitor lit up. The image of a duck flapped across the screen, towing a banner with words in bright red

63

letters: SNOOPERS BEWARE—THE PHAN-
TOM PROGRAMMER SEES ALL! Frank and
Joe burst out laughing.

"Gotcha!" Mike proclaimed, appearing in the
doorway with a wide grin on his face. Then the
grin faded. "What are you guys doing here?"
he demanded.

Joe gave Frank a glance that said, You take
it from here.

"We were surprised that you weren't at the
Project Planet Earth meeting after school this
afternoon," Frank said. "Erika gave a very interesting progress report."

"Anything newsworthy is bound to turn up
on my desk in the next day or two," Mike said
dryly. "Erika's an expert at tooting her own
horn."

"She may not want people to read about what
happened this afternoon," Joe told him. "All
the money the project raised last week, over
eight hundred dollars, vanished."

Mike was suddenly interested. "What do you
mean? Erika lost it? Somebody pinched it?"

"She was keeping it in a cash box in her
desk," Frank explained. "But when she opened
the box, all she found was a folded-up copy of
this week's *Review*. I see you've got a few copies
here," he added, going over to the bookcase and
picking up one of a small stack of newspapers.

"Careful with that paper," Mike said. "Those
are proof copies, and they're pretty smudgy."

Frank glanced down. His fingertips were

black with ink, and the photo of basketball star Chuck Franklin on page one was so smeared that he had to read the caption to recognize Chuck.

"You have a key to the student government office, don't you?" Joe asked.

"Sure," Mike replied. "So what?"

"And the desk that Erika's using, that used to be in the *Review* office, didn't it?" Joe continued. "She left the cash box locked in the drawer of that desk. You don't happen to have a key to it still, do you?"

Mike's ears reddened, but his voice stayed level, as he said, "As far as I know, I never had one. At the *Review* we don't usually lock our desks. We trust one another."

"The other week, at that first Project Planet Earth meeting, you made a speech about needing a more modern computer system," Frank said. "This one looks as modern as they come. Something you could use for your school stuff, too. Where did you get the money to buy it?"

Mike's eyes narrowed. "You know what, Frank?" he said in a voice that trembled slightly. "That is none of your business. And I'll tell you something else, too. You and your brother are so busy *playing* detective that you don't notice a major crime when it's going on right under your noses. You're in the wrong place, my friends. You'd better leave. I have a lot to do. The story I'm working on is one that'll blow this town wide open."

Joe gave a slight shrug, as if to say, If he doesn't want to talk to us, we can't force him.

Frank decided to give it one more try. "Somebody took that money, Mike," he said in a level voice. "I'm not saying you did it. But if you know anything that might help us track down the person who did do it, you should pass it on. An awful lot of us put in an awful lot of work last week to raise that money, and nobody is going to be very happy to find out that it's been stolen."

Mike turned to face the window. "I'm not happy about it, either," he said. "But believe it or not, I've got more important things on my mind."

Joe jumped in. "You mean like drawing ducks on your fancy new computer?"

Mike clenched his fists but kept his back turned to them. "You'll find out what I mean soon enough," he said. "Now, will you guys please go away and leave me alone?"

Frank took a pad and pen from his pocket. "Okay, Mike," he said, scribbling. "But I'm leaving you our phone numbers. The top one is our home, and the other one is the cellular phone in the van. If you think of anything, anything at all, you know how to get in touch with us. Come on, Joe, let's hit the road."

As they were walking to the van, a small, dusty car pulled up to the curb and flicked off its lights and B. J. Russo got out. He seemed surprised to see them. "Hey, guys, how's the detecting?" he called.

"Fine," Joe called back. "How's the computing?"

"Getting better all the time," B.J. replied with a grin. "See you."

He walked up to the door and rang. As Mrs. Tano let him in, Joe said, "I wonder how B.J. likes quacking ducks?"

"He's about to find out," Frank replied, getting into the van. "I wonder if we're following the wrong scent. What do we really have on Mike?"

"Nothing," Joe said. "But you remember what we used to say in third grade? 'There's no proof, but I've lost a dime and you just bought gum.' Project Planet Earth just lost eight hundred dollars, and Mike bought a computer that cost even more than that."

Frank frowned. "Yes, but he ordered it earlier. How could he have known that Erika was going to have all that cash lying around unguarded in a desk that he had a key for?"

"You're right, he couldn't have," Joe said. "But maybe he didn't plan to steal the money. Maybe he simply saw his chance and took it. Which means he couldn't have planned to pay for the computer with it. He must have had some other way to pay for it."

Frank said, "And *that* means that if he took the money, it might still be around somewhere.

Would he take it home with him? Or would he try to hide it at school?"

Joe glanced at his watch and said, "It doesn't matter. We can't search his house, and the school building is locked up for the night. Not only that, it's closed tomorrow, too, for Founders' Day. We'll have to wait until Wednesday morning."

Frank smacked his fist into his palm. "So far, this case isn't hanging together. I think something bigger than we realize is going on—much bigger than phony leaflets or even the theft of the money. Maybe Mike was serious about that big story he's after. What could we be missing?"

Joe started the engine. "We're missing dinner, for a start," he replied. "Let's call Mom, grab a hamburger, then get over to Vanessa's for our team meeting."

Vanessa and her mother, Andrea Bender, had moved to Bayport from New York City and now lived in a big farmhouse just outside of town. Mrs. Bender had turned an old barn on her property into a high-tech computer animation studio, where she created special effects for films and commercials.

When the Hardys arrived, Mrs. Bender opened the door. She was wearing a paint-stained sweatshirt and baggy jeans, and holding an open paperback in her left hand. "Hi, Joe, Frank," she said. "The rest of your group is back in the kitchen, sampling a new line of all-natural cookies. You know the way." She returned to the living room. Joe and Frank followed the sound of voices to the big country kitchen at the rear of the house.

"Here they are," Biff called, from his seat at the long, time-scarred table in the middle of the room.

Vanessa pushed out two chairs. "We were wondering if we should start without you," she said.

Frank asked, "What about Tony? Is he coming?"

Callie shook her head. "He called. The guy who was scheduled for the evening shift at Mr. Pizza is sick. We'll have to fill him in later."

"Before we get into our plans for this week," Vanessa said, "what about the missing money? Did you find out anything?"

"Not a lot," Joe confessed. He filled them in on what he and Frank had learned that afternoon, then concluded, "It's looking more and more like Lucy is guilty. The problem is, we don't have any evidence against her."

"That's where we come in," Chet announced. "We can take turns following her, until she makes a slip."

"I'm not sure that'll work," Frank replied. "If she knows she's being watched, she'll avoid doing anything incriminating. Besides, don't forget that tomorrow's a collection day. We can't follow Lucy and make our rounds."

"But what we can do," Joe added, "is keep

a sharp eye out for Project Planet Earth vans with muddy license plates."

"If we work at it," Frank said, "we'll nail whoever's doing it *and* beat our last week's total."

"That should be easy, now that Vanessa and her mom have finished these collection schedules," Callie said, holding up a leaflet decorated with cartoon characters. "Aren't they terrific?"

"We'll win that ski trip for sure," Chet said dreamily. "I can just imagine it—stacks of pancakes with real maple syrup and country sausage for breakfast, maple-cured baked ham and New England baked beans at supper, mugs of hot spiced cider in front of the fireplace just before bedtime. . . ."

"Aren't you forgetting something?" Callie asked with a laugh. "What about the skiing?"

The next morning as Frank was going down the stairs to breakfast, the telephone rang. His mother answered, then called to him. Putting her palm over the mouthpiece, she said, "It's Eleanor Tano, Michael's mother. She sounds very upset."

Frank took the receiver and said hello.

"I apologize for calling so early, and on a day off, too," Mrs. Tano said. "But I'm afraid I don't know where else to turn."

"What's the problem, Mrs. Tano?" Frank asked.

"It's Mike. He never came home last night. I

just found out—his bed wasn't slept in. He's never done that before. He would have called if he could. I'm so worried. Please—will you and your brother help me?"

"Of course we will," Frank said. "I'm sure everything's—"

"I know something's happened to Mike," Mrs. Tano interrupted. Frank heard a catch in her voice. "Something terrible."

Chapter

8

As soon as Frank got off the phone with Mike's mother, he called up to Joe and told him what had happened.

"I'll be right down," Joe called back. "But what about breakfast? I'm starved."

"We can eat it on the way," Frank replied. He went to the kitchen and put four slices of bread in the toaster, then fished two thermos bottles from a cabinet under the counter, rinsed them, and filled them with hot chocolate. Just as he finished and Joe entered the kitchen, the toast popped up.

"Butter and jam?" Frank asked.

"No, thanks." Joe opened the cabinet next to the stove and pulled out a jar of crunchy peanut butter. "For a quick start in the morning, it's PB and J every time."

Frank gave an exaggerated shudder and went on fixing his toast.

As they drove across town, Joe said, "Let's list the possibilities. If Mike's the bad guy, he may have dropped out of sight because he's up to something super-bad or because yesterday convinced him that we were onto him and he wanted to get away."

"And if he's a good guy?" Frank asked. He was curious to find out if he and Joe were thinking along the same lines.

"If he's a good guy, chances are that he made a dumb move and attracted the attention, maybe of the guys in the story he said he was checking out. They may have decided to take him out of the game, one way or another," Joe said.

"That's supposing there are 'bad guys' involved, that this case is bigger than the one at school," Frank pointed out. "But I'll go along with you for a minute. If he knew these 'bad guys' were after him, he might have dropped out of sight to escape them. Therefore, his goals, whatever they are, might be in total conflict with the goals of whoever gave us that death-defying ride across the bridge yesterday."

"Lucy, you mean," Joe said.

Frank frowned. "Not necessarily," he replied. "The evidence against Lucy does keep piling up, but so far all of it is pretty shaky. We need to keep an open mind."

Mike's front door swung open the moment

Joe and Frank pulled up to the curb. Mrs. Tano had obviously been watching for them.

"Am I glad to see you!" she said when they reached the door. "Please come in. It's cold out there."

"Still no word from Mike?" Frank asked as she closed the door behind them.

"No, nothing," she replied, pressing the back of her hand to her forehead. "I can't begin to tell you how worried I am. Oh—would you boys like anything? Some juice or cocoa?"

Joe answered for both of them. "No, thanks, Mrs. Tano. If Mike's in trouble, we don't want to waste any time finding him. When did you see him last?"

"Around seven last night," she said promptly. "A friend of his dropped by right after you boys left, but he didn't stay long. After the friend left, Mike came downstairs and said he had to go out. I tried to talk him into waiting until after dinner, but he said he had to do something that couldn't wait."

"He didn't say what it was?" Frank asked.

"Just that it was a really big story, the biggest he'd ever had a shot at," Mrs. Tano replied. "That's one reason I called you instead of the police. I know how Mike feels about his stories. If I did something that interfered with some important investigation he'd be very upset. But I couldn't sit back and do nothing, not knowing where he is."

"We'll do everything we can, Mrs. Tano,"

Frank assured her. "Do you remember what Mike was wearing when he went out last night?"

"He was wearing black jeans, a black turtle-neck, and his black leather jacket." A faint smile flickered across her face. "When I asked him if he was trying to look like a beatnik, he told me there hadn't been any beatniks since I was in kindergarten."

Joe asked, "Do you mind if we look around Mike's room? He might have left a clue where he was going."

"Please do," Mrs. Tano said. "You know the way."

Frank followed Joe up the stairs. Mike's room was exactly as it had been the afternoon before, except for the flannel shirt and jeans tossed on the bed. Frank noticed that the computer was still on. Did Mike leave it on all the time, as some power-users did, or had he expected to be back in a short time?

"That's what Mike was wearing when we saw him," Joe said, pointing to the clothes on the bed. "First question—why did he take the trouble to change?"

"Not for the sake of fashion," Frank replied with a short laugh. "I know wearing all black is a thing with some people, but Mike never struck me as one of them. I'd say he was planning to do something sneaky and wanted to cut down on the chances of being seen."

Joe nodded. "I'll buy that. The next question

is, *what* sneaky thing? Maybe he was nice enough to jot down his plans and leave them for us." He crossed to the desk and began to look through the papers on top.

Frank sat down at the computer and hit the space bar. The screen lit up, but no quacking duck followed. Instead, he saw an opening screen that resembled a desktop. If Mike was like most people with a new high-tech toy, he had probably already started to play with it. Frank used the mouse to move the tiny arrow over to the image of a file drawer, then clicked.

KEY WORD, PLEASE? appeared at the bottom of the screen. Frank gave a sigh. Mike had obviously locked his files with a password. What word would he have used? Any combination of letters at all, in principle, but most people chose a word they were sure of remembering. In quick succession Frank tried MIKE, TANO, MIKETANO, and MYFILES. None of them worked.

Frank sat back and stared, frustrated, at the screen. He didn't have time to pursue this particular puzzle any further, not with Mike missing. Was there anything else to be learned from the computer?

His eye fell on the icon of a desk calendar. Was that locked, too? He moved the arrow to it and clicked. A window opened on the calendar page for the day. At the top, in big letters, Frank read, "BAYPORT FOUNDERS DAY—NO SCHOOL—YAY!" No appointments were listed, but under "TO DO" were "PPE coll," "1st dr," and "call LV."

PPE was obviously Project Planet Earth, Frank thought, and today *was* collection day. Mike had also intended to start a first draft of some article, and to call LV—Lucy Velez? Interesting, but not terrifically helpful. In any case, Mike had gone missing the day before, not now. Frank checked the list of commands, then used the up arrow to change the calendar page to Monday.

There were only three entries. Under "TO DO," it said, "load files." Opposite 6:30 P.M. was "bj over-duck." Frank was sure he understood what that meant. And opposite 8:30 P.M. it said "UP!!!"

"Joe, come here a second. I think I've found something," Frank called.

Joe leaned on Frank's shoulder and peered at the screen. " 'Up,' " he read aloud. "Up where?"

"That's for Mike to know and us to figure out," Frank replied. "Uptown? Up north? Up a flagpole?"

Joe joined the guessing game, but after half a dozen more suggestions, he said, "What if it isn't 'up,' what if it's somebody's initials? Do we know anybody whose initials are *UP?*"

Frank thought for a moment, then said, "I don't think I do, but Mike might." He grabbed the mouse and moved the arrow to the address book icon, then clicked through to the *P*s. The "page" was blank.

"No good," he said. "Did you notice an address book on his desk?"

Joe crossed the room. A moment later he said, "Nope. And you know what? The only first name I can think of that starts with *u* is Ursula, and I've never actually met anybody named Ursula. Maybe *UP* isn't a person. Maybe it's a place, like University Park."

"Or 'usual place,'" Frank contributed. "As in, 'Meet me at the usual place.' Face it, we could play guessing games for the rest of the morning. What do we know for sure? We know that Mike left the house last night, and that he was wearing all black."

"And we know that he wrote in *UP* for eight-thirty, and that he didn't come home," Joe added. "So where does that leave us?"

Frank straightened up, struck by a sudden idea. *"U . . . P,"* he said slowly. "United Plastics—UniPlast! Of course! Mike must have planned to sneak into the UniPlast factory last night. And while he was there, something must have happened to keep him from coming home."

"It makes sense," Joe said, nodding. "But why would he want to sneak into the UniPlast plant?"

"If he's the one who's trying to wreck Project Planet Earth, he probably meant to carry out some kind of dirty trick," Frank replied. "And if he isn't the one, he may have had the idea of finding evidence against the person who is. Maybe that's the big story he told us about. But the best way to answer that question is to check out the plant to see what we can turn up. Come on, let's roll."

Fifteen minutes later they pulled up at the entrance to the UniPlast factory. The gate was closed. Beyond, the parking lot was practically empty. A gray-haired man stepped out of the gatekeeper's booth and walked over to the van.

"Sorry, boys, the plant is closed for the holiday," he said. "You'll have to come back tomorrow."

"But we're with the high school recycling project," Frank quickly replied. "We were told we could pick up more plastic receptacles to pass out to people around town. We really need them for this afternoon."

"Oh?" The watchman took off his cap and scratched his head. "Nobody told me about it, but I know we're supposed to help you any way we can. Do you know where to find them?"

"Sure," Frank said. "They're in the room next to the recycling center's loading dock. I know the way."

"Well . . . okay," the man finally said. "But don't touch anything. Some of the machines in that recycling operation are pretty dangerous."

"We won't," Frank promised. The watchman swung the gate open. Frank gave him a wave as he drove past.

At the loading dock Frank parked the van, and he and Joe got out. The big sliding doors were closed, but a smaller door to one side was ajar. Inside, only a couple of weak lights were burning.

"What now?" Joe asked in a low voice.

"We look around," Frank replied. "And if you find the light switches, turn them on."

Joe turned to the left and began to circle the room. Frank went to the right. He had only gone a few steps when his toe banged into something hard that rolled away. He bent down and picked up a metal flashlight. The lens was cracked, and nothing happened when he moved the switch. On the cap, in faded black marker, were the letters *M* and *T*.

Frank hurried over to Joe and showed him his find. "Mike was here," he said. "Something startled him enough to make him drop his flashlight, and whatever happened next, he never came back for it. I don't like this, Joe."

Frank scanned the room. Against the wall, near the door that led to the main recycling area, were several of the metal drums he had noticed on his earlier visit. Was there a space behind them? Frank tried to move one of the drums out of the way, but it was too heavy to budge. As he was turning away, he noticed something white on the ground between two of the drums. It was that week's *Review,* a smudged proof copy like those he and Joe had seen in Mike's room the day before. Now he was positive that Mike had come here the night before.

"Frank," Joe said. "There's a light under that door."

Frank joined his brother as he gingerly turned the knob and pushed the door open.

"Anybody here?" Joe called. The only answer was his own voice, echoing off the walls.

Frank peered around the large, warehouselike room. To the right, a conveyor belt led from a door in the wall past four large metal bins on wheels. The bins were labeled Type I, Type II, and so on, and were filled with different kinds of used plastic containers. The conveyor belt ended at a larger bin with the word *unusable* painted on its side.

In the center of the room was a machine at least eight feet tall and nearly as wide. It looked like some sort of stamping press. Several bales of compressed plastic, each one about eight feet thick, were stacked on a pallet next to it. On the machine's control panel, a light glowed red.

Joe took a couple of steps to the left, examining the huge machine. Suddenly he turned pale. "Frank!" he said. "Look!"

Frank looked and felt his stomach turn over. Protruding from the far side of the baling machine was a black shoe—and a few inches of a khaki-clad leg.

Chapter

9

JOE RISKED ONE GLANCE as the paramedics lifted the rubberized body bag onto a rolling stretcher. Then he turned away and swallowed.

"His name was Vic Krieger," Officer Con Riley said, opening his notebook. Officer Riley had known Frank and Joe and their detective father for a long time and was used to answering their questions. "According to the guy at the gate, he was some kind of special security guard. He clocked in yesterday just before four and was supposed to go off duty at midnight. He didn't, though. I found his card next to the time clock, unpunched."

Frank cleared his throat. "Does that mean he died sometime between four and midnight?" he asked.

Riley considered for a moment, then shook

his head. "Not necessarily. He may have had some reason for sticking around after his shift was over. But that fits well enough with the medical examiner's estimated time of death. We'll know more after the autopsy."

"You know," Joe said tentatively, "it must have happened after hours on Monday, or someone would have found him before we did. And when the plant was in operation, someone would have been running the machine, right?"

"That's another thing else we have to check out," Riley replied. "I also want somebody to explain to me how Krieger fell into that machine while it was running."

He shook his head. "You fellows have a gift for turning up at the wrong place at the right time, don't you?" he continued. "Tell me again what you were doing here when the plant was closed."

Frank explained about Project Planet Earth and the need to get more collection bins. He did not mention Mike Tano's name. He and Joe had no positive proof that Mike had come to the plant the evening before—the initials on the broken flashlight could be pure coincidence— and it didn't seem right to drag someone into a police investigation on the basis of a hunch.

The detective in charge was a heavyset, gray-haired man named William Broussard, who had recently moved to Bayport from Louisiana. This was Frank and Joe's first contact with him. He came over and told Con Riley, "The photographer's almost done. Let's wrap it up here and get a head start on the paperwork."

"What exactly happened?" Joe asked.

Instead of answering directly, Broussard said, "I've heard of you two. You've done some pretty clever detecting, from what they say. Well, the police always welcome the cooperation of the public, but if you come across any facts that bear on a case of mine, you bring them straight to me. No amateur investigating, you hear? Because if I get the idea you're interfering with my work, you'll be sorry, I guarantee."

Con Riley said, "I don't think you need to worry about Joe and Frank. They've always been very responsible, as well as helpful."

"As long as they know where we all stand," Broussard replied. "Now—"

He broke off as a car braked violently to a stop just outside the loading bay. A door was opened and slammed just before someone came running up the steps and flung open the door. Joe recognized Sol Stone.

"Who's in charge here?" Stone demanded loudly. "I want a full report, at once!"

Joe noticed Detective Broussard's lips tighten into a straight line. "And who might you be?" the detective asked in a deceptively calm voice.

Stone seemed to realize that he had made an error. More calmly, he introduced himself, then added, "I got a phone call that there'd been a death at the plant, so I came right over. Who died, and how?"

"One of the guards, a guy named Krieger," Officer Riley replied. He pointed with his thumb to the machine in the center of the room. "He was crushed by that monster over there."

The blood drained from Stone's face. "The baler? How awful!" he said. He shook his head slowly. "I blame myself for this. I hired Krieger to help protect some of our research projects. I suppose whoever briefed him on the plant didn't impress him with the need to be careful around the machinery."

"If that machine is so dangerous, why isn't it fenced off in some way?" Frank asked.

Stone peered at him with just a trace of recognition in his eyes. "What are you doing here?" he demanded. "This facility is closed today. I must ask you to leave at once."

Frank checked with Joe, then Con Riley, who gave an almost imperceptible nod.

"Sure, Mr. Stone," he said. "Whatever you say."

Frank and Joe turned and left the recycling center through the door into the loading area. Joe glanced over his shoulder. Stone and Broussard were next to the baling machine. From Broussard's gestures, it was obvious that he was explaining to the company head how Krieger's death had happened.

Just then Joe heard a loud, grating noise. Daylight flooded the loading bay as the doors to the dock opened. Joe saw that a dark blue truck had backed up to the dock. Two men in blue coveralls came in. The taller of them was wearing a wide weight lifter's leather belt around his waist. They nodded to Joe and Frank, then went over to the metal drums near the wall. Pulling on a pair of heavy work gloves, the shorter man grabbed the rim of one of the drums with both hands, then leaned back with all his weight. The drum didn't budge.

His partner said, "Cut it out, Ed, before you bust something. I'll go find us a forklift."

Stone appeared in the doorway to the recycling center. "What are you men doing here?" he asked sharply. "Didn't the guard tell you the plant is closed? It's a holiday."

"Not for us, it isn't," the guy with the weight lifter's belt replied. "Our dispatcher told us to come get this stuff, so that's what we're doing."

"I see. Very well." Stone looked over his shoulder and said to Riley and Broussard, "Would you gentlemen like to continue our conversation in my office? We won't be disturbed there."

He turned back and noticed that Joe and Frank were still there. He blinked in surprise and opened his mouth to yell at them, but Joe gave him a casual wave and started out the door with Frank right behind. Zipping up their jackets against the cold, they edged past the truck. Joe noticed that the company name on its side had been painted over. Next to the truck was a gleaming red German sports sedan with a vanity license plate that read UNIPLAST.

Joe chuckled and said, "Three guesses whose car that is."

Frank laughed. "Do I win the car if I get it right? What I want to know," he continued, "is why those two guys are collecting those drums when the plant's supposed to be closed."

"Their boss probably didn't realize it was closed," Joe suggested. "Nobody outside of town celebrates Bayport Founders' Day."

"Maybe," Frank said doubtfully as Joe got into the van. "But I'm jotting down the license number of the truck, just in case."

As they drove home, Frank shook his head, gazing out the window at the passing scenery. "I'm worried about Mike," he said. "We found two clues—the paper and the flashlight—that say he was at the plant last night. For all we know, he was there when Krieger was killed."

"Hold on," Joe said. "What are you trying to say? Krieger's death was an accident."

"A pretty strange accident," Frank retorted. "I'm not saying Mike had anything to do with it. But I would like to know why he was at the plant and what he saw, if anything. Let's call his mom when we get home. Maybe she's heard from him."

When they walked into the house, they found their aunt Gertrude in the kitchen, finishing up preparing a pot of chili. "I had a feeling you wouldn't miss lunch," she said. "It's so cold today, I thought chili would warm you up. Go wash your hands and come to the table. Oh—somebody called earlier. I didn't get to the phone in time, but I think they left a message."

Joe followed Frank to the hallway. Aunt Gertrude was right—the message light on the answering machine was blinking. Frank pressed Playback and heard Mrs. Tano's voice.

"Thanks for trying to help, but I don't want you to waste any more time looking for my son," she said. Her voice trembled with fear. "Everything is all right. I'm so sorry I bothered you this morning." The machine clicked off.

Joe picked up the phone and dialed Mike's number. He held the receiver so Frank could listen, too. When Mrs. Tano answered, all she would say was, "I'm sorry, I can't talk to you. Goodbye."

Joe raised an eyebrow at Frank. "Is my voice that scary?" he asked, hanging up.

"No, but something sure is scaring her," Frank replied. "Earlier Mike's mom was terrified that Mike was lost. Now she sounds even more terrified that we might manage to find him."

Joe sighed. "This is too confusing for me," he said. "Let's go eat lunch. We've got a lot of plastic to pick up this afternoon."

Frank checked for Mike in English class the next morning, but he wasn't there. The situation seemed grim. Maybe Con Riley had some news,

Frank thought. After third period Frank put in a call to the officer.

"Hi, Frank," Riley said when Frank got through to him. "I bet you're wondering about that poor guy you and Joe found yesterday. Doc says he probably died between seven and ten P.M. There was nothing unusual to show that it wasn't an accident. We'll check out everything, of course, but I'd be surprised if they find out anything more."

"What kind of guy was Krieger?" Frank asked.

"Don't quote me, but he wasn't anyone you'd want to hang with," Riley replied. "A loner, no real friends, got into arguments often and fights now and then. No criminal record as far as we know, but from what I learned talking to people who knew him, that was just a matter of time."

"He doesn't sound like the best choice for a security guard," Frank observed.

Riley laughed. "Depends. If you want to hire muscle, he might have been a good choice. Brains and diplomacy, I'd have to say no."

"Oops, I have to run or I'll be late for class," Frank said. "One last thing—would you mind tracking down a license plate for me?"

When Frank finished reading off the number he had copied from the blue truck the day before, Con Riley said, "I'm not sure what the regulations say about this, but if I'm sitting at the computer, my fingers might twitch in that direction. And if there's anything to pass along,

I might just casually mention it to you, in passing."

"Thanks," Frank said with a laugh. "I'll let you know if it leads anywhere."

At lunchtime in the cafeteria, Frank and Joe told their friends about Mike's disappearance and the death of the special guard at UniPlast.

"You don't really think that Mike had anything to do with that guy's death, do you?" Callie demanded.

"I can't answer yes or no," Frank responded. "We found a couple of clues that point to Mike being on the scene at the right time. That's it, really, as far as hard evidence goes. But it's not hard to come up with a reasonable scenario."

Joe took up the story. "Suppose we're right, that Mike was snooping around the plant last night. That's exactly what this Krieger was hired to stop. So let's say he spotted Mike and chased him into the recycling center. They struggled, and somehow Krieger fell into the crushing machine, which went on."

"Don't!" Vanessa exclaimed, covering her face with her hands. "I can't stand to even imagine it!"

"Sorry," Joe replied. "But anyway, as soon as Mike realized what had happened, he went into hiding. Then, at some point yesterday, he got in touch with his mother and convinced her to call us off his trail."

Tony paused with his tuna on toast halfway to his mouth and said, "It hangs together, it really does. So what next? Did you guys do any more investigating yesterday?"

Frank shook his head. "Nope. Joe and I spent the afternoon collecting plastic. Besides, we weren't sure where to go next." He looked around the table. "Any ideas?" he asked.

Biff frowned. "Well ... if Mike sneaked into the UniPlast factory to sabotage our project, does that mean he's behind the phony leaflets, too?" he asked. "What if we find proof that he wrote them? We could look for a backup file on the student council computer or something like that."

Joe was taking notes. "Good," he said, jotting down Biff's idea. "What else?"

"I know some of Mike's friends," Chet offered. "I'll hunt them down and talk to them. Maybe I can find out something useful."

"Chet—Mike's pals," Joe said as he wrote.

"I think we need to know if other teams have been sabotaged, or if it's only us," Callie said. "Why don't I survey the other teams?"

"Good idea," Frank said. "I think we're getting somewhere now."

"What about the newspaper office?" Vanessa asked. "Isn't it possible that Mike left some clue to his plans there?"

"It's worth checking out," Joe said, giving her an encouraging smile. He glanced at his watch. "In fact, why don't we do it right now? We have just enough time before next period."

As they were returning their trays, Joe

peeked over his shoulder at Frank. "You come, too," he said, winking. "There's nothing like the prestige of a senior to smooth the way."

Frank laughed and aimed a punch at his brother's arm. As usual, it missed by a hair.

The door to the *Review* office stood open. Joe tapped at it anyway, then put his head inside. Four students were absorbed in what looked like proofs of the paper, and a couple more were examining black-and-white photographs in one corner of the room.

A girl in a yellow turtleneck and baggy blue corduroy overalls looked up from the computer terminal near the door. "Can I help you?" she asked, brushing her hair back from her eyes.

Joe introduced himself, Frank, and Vanessa.

"Oh, sure, I've heard of you," the girl said. "I'm Valerie Shoemaker. What's up?"

Joe said, "Mike Tano kind of dropped out of sight on Monday, and his mother asked us to help her track him down. You don't happen to know where he is, do you?"

"I wish I did," Valerie said with barely hidden irritation. "We've got a paper to put out, and this is my very first semester working on it. I'm supposed to be in charge of the features section, but I can't do it all myself. Even if I did, I don't suppose Mike would like the result very much."

"Is he difficult to work with?" Vanessa asked.

Valerie turned pink. "I didn't say that," she replied. "No, it's just—well, we don't always agree about things going on around school. But he's a senior, and the editor in chief, and I'm just a lowly sophomore assistant editor, so I don't have to tell you whose ideas show up in the *Review,* do I?"

Frank smiled sympathetically and said, "We'd like to check around the office a little to see if we can find clues to explain what's happened to Mike. Is that okay?"

A look of alarm crossed Valerie's face. "I don't think I have the authority to . . ." she began.

"We'll take full responsibility," Vanessa said in a soothing voice. "And you can stay with us the whole time."

"Mike could be in some kind of trouble, Valerie," Frank added seriously. "We may be able to help him, *if* we can find him."

Valerie threw up her hands. "Okay, then," she said. "That's Mike's desk, over there in the corner."

The rest of the staff seemed too busy to notice as they crossed the room. Frank handed Vanessa a stack of papers form the top of the desk, then began to leaf through another stack himself. Joe pulled open the top drawer on the right. All it contained were paper clips, rubber bands, chewed-up ballpoint pens, and a couple of notepads. He tried the second drawer.

"Frank? Vanessa? Look at this," he said, quietly but urgently. He pointed to a thick manila envelope with "PPE–1st wk" scrawled on the front.

"Open it," Frank said, crowding closer.

Joe unfastened the flap and turned the envelope upside down. Out tumbled a thick wad of ten- and twenty-dollar bills.

Chapter
10

FRANK STARED at the stack of money tumbling onto Mike's desk and gave a low whistle. "Looks like we just found the missing cash," he said. "We'd better let Erika know right away."

"I'll go find her," Vanessa offered, and hurried away.

Valerie was staring at the money, as if hypnotized. "Is that the money that was taken from Project Planet Earth?" she asked.

"If it isn't, it's a really good imitation," Joe replied, as some of the staff members watched them from their desks.

"But how did it get into Mike's desk drawer?" Valerie continued.

"That's a very good question," Frank said. He was about to say more, but at that moment

Erika came rushing in, with Vanessa right behind her.

"You found it," Erika exclaimed. "Wonderful! Where was it?"

Joe told her. Her eyes widened.

"Mike?" she said. "I know he didn't agree with everything we were doing, but I never dreamed he'd try to wreck the project by stealing our money."

"Now, hold on," Valerie objected. "Mike Tano is no thief, and anyone who says so is a liar."

"Frank and Joe found the money in his desk," Erika pointed out. "What are we supposed to think?"

" 'Supposed to think.' That's just the point," Valerie promptly replied. "Somebody's trying to make you think that Mike's a crook. It's a frame. That's the only possible answer."

"But why?" Vanessa asked.

Valerie hesitated. "Maybe they don't like something he wrote," she said. "If people start to think he's dishonest, they won't pay attention to what he writes."

Frank had been holding back, to see what the others had to say. Now he decided it was time to step in. "Erika? What if we hadn't found the money here? Do you have any other reason to think that Mike might want to wreck Project Planet Earth?"

Erika blinked. "Some people will do anything to discredit us," she said. "I've heard rumors that several big companies want to do away with the town's recycling program. Right now it's easy for them to ignore federal recycling laws, and it costs them a lot of money to respect the environment. If our project is a big success, Bayport's recycling record will be in the spotlight, and that's the last thing those big companies would want. Their slipshod ways would be discovered. Maybe Mike was working for one of them."

"Don't be ridiculous!" Valerie snapped. "Mike and I may not see eye-to-eye on everything, but he's honest."

"Sure, sure," Erika said hastily. "I shouldn't have said that. Well, then, maybe one of those big companies was afraid of what he might write about them and decided to frame him."

"It's possible," Joe said. "But don't forget, it wasn't a big company that sneaked into the student government office and stole eight hundred dollars, then hid it in Mike's desk. It was a *person*—probably a student, somebody we know. The question is, who?"

From the hallway came the sound of a bell.

"Oh, no, I'm late again!" Valerie cried. "Ms. Harcel is going to kill me! I'm sorry, you guys have to clear out, so I can lock up the office."

Frank noticed that most of the staff had already left.

As they walked into the hallway, Erika said, "I have to run, too. I'm taking this envelope straight to the school office for safekeeping."

Frank arranged to meet Joe and Vanessa outside the student government office right after school. Then the three hurried to their classes.

Frank and Joe arrived at the meeting place at the same time and stepped over against the wall, out of the way of the crowd of students making their way toward the exits.

"I've been thinking," Joe said in an undertone. "Why would Mike leave all that cash in an unlocked desk drawer? I don't know if he's honest or not, but I know he's not stupid. I think that Valerie was right. This has to be an attempt to frame him."

Frank nodded. "I'm with you on that, but there's something more. Whoever put the money there must have counted on someone besides Mike finding it. After all, if Mike had found it he might have just turned it in, and then the frame wouldn't have worked. Does that mean the thief *knew* that Mike was going to be missing and that someone—us, for instance—was likely to go through his desk?"

Vanessa came up as Frank was saying this. She frowned. "But nobody knew Mike was missing until yesterday morning," she pointed out. "And the school was closed yesterday. That means the money must have been hidden in Mike's drawer sometime this morning."

"It could have been put there on Monday by somebody who knew that Mike was *going* to be missing," Joe said. "Which means, either somebody knew his plans ahead of time, or somebody was planning to kidnap him."

"Whoa!" Frank said. "I've got a feeling we're adding two plus two and getting twenty-two. What do we actually know? The money was taken from the cash box between noon and three on Monday. For practically all that time, it was locked in a desk drawer in the student government office, and there was someone in the office. Monday evening Mike apparently sneaked into the UniPlast plant, and nobody's seen him since as far as we know. And today the missing money has turned up in Mike's desk drawer."

"When was it put there?" Vanessa asked.

"Good question," Frank replied. "Either sometime on Monday—maybe as soon as it was stolen—or sometime this morning. If it was this morning, that probably lets Mike off the hook. He hasn't been here today."

"As far as we know," Joe added. "He could have sneaked into the *Review* office, then split. Hey, wait—it must have been today. Remember? When we were in the *Review* office on Monday afternoon, the guy who took our message for Mike rummaged around in Mike's drawers to find a pen. If the envelope with the money had been there then, he would have noticed it. And the guy left right after we did and he told us he had to lock the office. So unless the person who put the money there has a key to the *Review* office, he or she must have put it there today."

"Let's go find out when the office opened today," Joe suggested.

Valerie was in the *Review* office, as was the guy Frank and Joe had spoken to on Monday. Valerie introduced him as Andre, then asked, "Have you found out who's trying to frame Mike?"

After an awkward hesitation, Frank said, "No, but we're doing our best to find out what happened." He explained what they wanted to know.

Valerie and Andre exchanged a doubtful glance. Then Valerie said, "I was here for half an hour during fourth period, and then again during lunch. But you guys are the nonstaff members who came in during those times."

"Was the door locked both times you came?" Vanessa asked.

Valerie thought hard. "I can't swear to it, but I'm sure I would have noticed if it wasn't."

"Did you lock the door when you left?" Joe asked.

"Of course I did," Valerie replied. "I wouldn't take a chance on someone making off with our computer. It may be pretty old and slow, but it's still worth something."

"And it's all we've got," Andre added.

"Were you here earlier today?" Frank asked Andre.

"I dropped by once, at about eleven, to see

if Mike was here," he replied. "And, yes, the door was locked, and, yes, I relocked it when I left."

Joe asked, "How many people have keys?"

Andre and Valerie exchanged another glance. Joe wondered if there was more to the exchange than simply deciding who would answer the question.

"I'm not sure," Andre said. "About half a dozen, I'd guess. All the 'key people.' Oh, sorry—bad joke. Mike probably has a list somewhere."

"Does Lucy Velez have a key?" Vanessa asked.

Valerie was baffled. "Why would she? She doesn't have anything to do with the paper."

Vanessa shook her head. "I was just wondering."

"Mike told us on Monday that he was working on a really important story," Frank said. "Can either of you tell us what it's about?"

Andre and Valerie both shook their heads. "Mike wouldn't let us in on anything like that," Andre explained. "Not until he had the whole thing ready to put to bed."

"That means about to be printed," Valerie added.

Joe was struck by a sudden recollection. He dug around in his backpack and found the list he had made on Monday of people who had keys to the student government office. He quickly scanned it, then turned to Valerie.

"You're active in student government, aren't you?"

"That's right," Valerie replied. "I'm sophomore class secretary. Why?"

"And you have a key to the student government office?" Joe continued.

"That's right," she said again. "What about it?"

"Somebody took that eight hundred dollars from a desk in the student government office and put it in a desk in here," Joe replied. "And it looks as if whoever did it had to have keys to both offices. One person who fits that description is Mike. You're another. Do you know of any others?"

Valerie glared at him as if he were something that had just crawled out of the kitchen drain. "I'm not answering any more questions," she declared coldly. "Mike had nothing to do with that missing money, and neither did I. Now, will you creeps clear out and let us get on with our work?"

Joe glanced at Frank, then Vanessa. "We're just trying to find out the truth," he told Valerie. "It can't hurt anybody but the guilty. Think about it."

He headed for the door with Vanessa and Frank close behind him. As he left the room, he called out, "See you." Valerie and Andre didn't reply, or even raise their heads.

"It's a good thing you're not running for office," Vanessa cracked. "That'd be two votes you just lost."

"Aw, come on," Joe said. He was feeling picked on. "We had to ask about those keys."

Vanessa slipped her arm into his. "I'm just teasing you, silly. What's next on the program?"

Joe thought for a minute. "If Mike really did go out to the UniPlast factory on Monday, somebody might have seen him. We should ask around there. After that, our recycling team is supposed to get together and compare notes."

"I'll call Aunt Gertrude. If any of the team members try to call us, she can tell them to come over around six," Frank offered.

As he walked off, Joe asked Vanessa, "Do you really think I was too rough on Andre and Valerie?"

"Well—you could have been more diplomatic," she replied. "You know the old saying about catching more flies with honey than with vinegar."

"Oh, is *that* what that means?" Joe joked. "I always thought it meant that honey is so gooey that the flies get stuck in it!"

Frank came back before Vanessa could do more than wrinkle her nose at Joe.

The UniPlast factory was in full operation that day, and Joe had to circle the parking lot to find an empty space. Then he, Frank, and Vanessa hiked across the lot to the loading dock, climbed the stairs, and went inside.

The loading dock was nearly empty, but Frank could hear the roar of the recycling machines next door. A worker pushing a hand truck loaded with crates of plastic into the loading bay noticed the group and jerked his thumb back over his shoulder. "The recycling center's through there," he said.

"We know," Joe told him, trying not to recall the last time he had been there. "We wondered if—"

He broke off as a man in a hard hat and light blue overalls entered the loading bay from the outer door. The name badge over his left pocket read Andersen. Two uniformed guards were right behind him. When the man saw Frank he stopped in his tracks and pointed Frank out to the guards.

"That kid—he had a tussle with Vic Krieger. Maybe the cops will want to talk to him. Grab him while I call them!"

Chapter

11

THE TWO GUARDS DREW their nightsticks as Andersen hurried to a telephone on the wall. Frank cautiously took one step forward.

"This is all a misunderstanding," he said in as calm a voice as he could. "I'm not here to make trouble. I'm with the high school recycling program. Andersen knows that, too. He made Krieger apologize to me the other day."

"Stay right where you are, fella," the older of the two guards said, refusing to listen to Frank. He moved a little to the left, while his partner moved to the right. They stopped on either side of Frank, about a yard away, bouncing their clubs in their palms.

"Joe? Shouldn't we do something?" Vanessa asked.

Joe nodded and said, "We should stand still

and not do anything that might make them nervous."

"Good advice, kid," the older guard remarked. "Andersen's got his eye out for you high school hoodlums. Ever since your project got started, he says weird things have been going on here."

Just then Frank heard a shout coming from outside the loading bay. "What the blazes is it this time?" the voice demanded loudly. "How am I supposed to run a company when— Oh. It's you again. I should have guessed."

Sol Stone stood in the doorway with his hands on his hips, glaring at Frank and Joe. Andersen hurried over and said something to him in a voice too low for Frank to hear.

Stone waved him aside. "Krieger's death was nothing but a stupid accident. The cops know that, and so do I, but I don't want those kids in my plant. If I see them here again, the turkey who let them past the gate is going to be finding the address of the nearest unemployment office, and so is his supervisor. Is that clear?"

"Yes, Mr. Stone," Andersen said, turning pale.

"Good." Stone turned to the guards. "Escort these troublemakers off the grounds, right now."

"Yes, sir," the older guard said sharply, and glared at Frank. "That means move it, buddy."

The two guards followed Frank, Joe, and Vanessa to the van, then walked behind the van to the main gate. As they drove away, Frank observed them talking to the watchman on the gate, gesturing in the direction of the van.

"From now on, we'd better let Biff, Callie, and the others bring in whatever we collect," Joe said.

The next day right after school Callie and Vanessa beat the Hardys home and were chatting with Fenton Hardy when Frank and Joe arrived.

"I'll be in my study if you need me for anything," Fenton said, getting to his feet. "Oh, and Con Riley called. I took a message—something about a truck you wanted traced. Is this anything to do with the case you're working on now?"

"I hope so," Frank said. "Thanks, Dad." He glanced at the slip of paper his father had handed him. All it said was "RJ Transport, Bayport Indust. Pk." and a phone number. Frank tucked it in his pocket. Then after his father had left, he told Callie about their visit to UniPlast the day before. "I have no problem with what Andersen did," Frank said, "but Stone is obviously building a major grudge against me and Joe. All because he found us at his plant two times. Oh, well—what about you? What did you learn yesterday and today?"

Callie pulled a couple of folded looseleaf pages from her purse, glanced at them, then said, "I managed to talk to people from six different teams. Five of them had the same kind of problems we did on Tuesday—empty bins and fake notes telling people that the campaign had been canceled. And one team last Tuesday found that someone had taken away the containers, too. That was on the south side."

"Unbelievable," Vanessa said. "What did the team members do?"

Callie shrugged. "They talked the guys at the plant into giving them a new batch of containers, then took them around again, house by house. They weren't happy about the extra work, I can tell you."

"So the sabotage isn't aimed specifically at our team," Joe pointed out. "That makes me feel a little better, I guess."

Frank said, "But you said that five of the six teams you talked to had suffered from dirty tricks. What about the sixth?"

"That's one of the interesting points," Callie replied. "Not only has one of the teams not had any trouble of that sort, it also happens to be well in the lead for that ski weekend. Anybody care to guess whose team it is?"

An image flashed through Frank's mind of a green minivan trying to force the Hardys' van off the bridge being driven by someone with big sunglasses and a dark ponytail. He was opening his mouth to say "Lucy Velez," when Vanessa beat him to it.

"You got it," Callie told Vanessa. "And I

think they're so far ahead because they've been stealing stuff from other people's routes."

"That's possible," Joe said. "But don't forget, there are at least twenty more teams to contact."

"Besides," Vanessa said, "it'd be awfully hard to keep something like that a secret."

"Not necessarily," Frank said. "It could be one person who's doing the whole thing—passing out the phony leaflets and stealing recyclables from other teams at the same time. The other members of the team may not even know about it. They might be surprised that they're doing so well, but I doubt if they'd spend much time figuring out the reason. Why argue with success?"

The doorbell rang. Joe went to answer it and returned with Chet.

"I think I've got something," Chet announced, even before he sat down. "Any of you know Bob Portago? He and Mike have been friends since kindergarten. Last week Mike told him that he was working on a really hot story. He said he was sure he could talk the Bayport paper into running it, and even hoped that one of the New York dailies would pick it up for their regional edition."

"Wow," Vanessa said, impressed. "That's like a pitcher on the Bayport High baseball team getting picked for a major league farm team!"

"Did Bob give you any leads to what this hot story might be about?" Frank asked.

Chet shook his head. "He didn't have a clue," he replied. "All Mike would tell him was that there were powerful interests involved. According to Mike, these interests would stop at nothing to keep the story from coming out. At the time Bob thought that maybe Mike had been watching too many TV shows about crusading reporters. But when I told him that Mike had disappeared, he started to wonder."

Chet paused impressively, then added, "The thing is, Mike told Bob that if these powerful interests heard that he was onto them, he might have to go into hiding to keep from being silenced."

Frank jumped to his feet. "Great work, Chet," he said. "But I think Joe and I had better question Bob, too. He may know something about Mike that he doesn't realize he knows, if you see what I mean. I don't think we should wait. Maybe Mike did go into hiding to keep out of the clutches of these powerful interests, whoever they are. But there's another possibility. He may be in their clutches already!"

Chet, Callie, and Vanessa quickly decided to fan out to see what they could find out about who was emptying other teams' bins. Joe scribbled a note to Biff and Tony, then he and Frank drove over to Bob Portago's house. Bob's mother directed them to a workshop over the garage. Bob, a short, stocky redhead, was up there sitting at a brilliantly lit workbench with a weird set of goggles over his eyes. When Frank tapped on the door, he pushed the goggles up onto his forehead and walked over to them.

"I know you," he announced. "You're Frank and Joe Hardy. Come on in. This is about Mike, isn't it?"

"That's right," Frank said. He and Joe followed Bob inside. On the workbench, shining in the light of a fluorescent lamp, was a tiny model of an old train engine.

"Hey, that is really something," Joe exclaimed. "Did you make it yourself?"

"Mostly," Bob replied. "It's a scale model of a Baldwin Four-Four-Two steam locomotive. The railroads used to use them to pull coal trains a hundred cars long through the Appalachian Mountains."

He showed them some of the delicate tools he used in making the models, then turned on a light over a glass-fronted cabinet. Inside, dozens of tiny locomotives and railroad cars were lined up on tracks less than a quarter of an inch apart.

"But you're not here to look at my model trains," he said. "You want to talk to me about Mike. I wish I could help, but I already told Chet everything I knew."

"Let's go over it again," Frank suggested. "You may remember some detail that slipped your mind when you were talking to Chet."

"Well, okay," Bob said doubtfully. He repeated his story. Frank listened carefully but couldn't find anything new in it.

"And you didn't get any idea of what Mike's story was about?" Frank asked.

"Just that it was a big story that people would sit up and notice," Bob replied. "For all I know, it could be anything from teachers' selling grades to a financial scam involving the most important bank in town."

"But Mike said that the people involved in this story might force him to go into hiding?" asked Joe.

Bob nodded. "That's right. I thought he was, like, being dramatic. Now I'm not so sure."

"Do you have any idea *where* he might hide?" Joe continued.

"He didn't give me the slightest hint," Bob replied. "After Chet left, I tried to remember every word Mike said. I know he didn't say anything about where he'd go."

"You've known Mike a long time, haven't you?" Frank said.

"Since we were four or five," Bob replied.

"Think back," Frank urged him. "Can you remember anything, from way back, that might give you a clue where Mike might hide?"

Bob focused in the distance. His silence stretched out so long that Frank began to wonder if he had forgotten they were there.

Suddenly he blinked and said, "Our shack— sure, he could be there!"

"What shack?" Joe asked quickly.

"You know Mike's house?" Bob said. "It's got thick woods in back of it. They belong to the water board, and it's strictly no trespassing, but when Mike and I were little, we used to play there all the time. One time we discovered this old shack with bushes all around it. It didn't look as if anybody had been there in years. We spent a whole summer fixing it up and playing fort. Then, the next summer, I went off to camp and we kind of forgot about it. But I bet it's still there, unless it's fallen down."

Frank knew this was an important lead. "Do you think we could find it?" he asked excitedly.

"I don't know," Bob said slowly. "There used to be a path that started just behind Mike's house. But I'm not sure it's still there."

"Let's say we find the path. What then?" Joe asked.

Bob stared at the corner of the ceiling and said, "You go in about a hundred fifty feet—maybe more—and look off to your left. There's a big thicket with a tall pine tree growing up out of the middle. That's where the shack is. You may have to crawl under the bushes to get to it, though. That's what makes it such a nifty hideout."

"We'll give it a try," Frank said.

Bob nodded. "I'd show you myself, but I have to go out with my parents. Some old friends of theirs are having a party. I have to go change in a few minutes."

"That's okay," Frank said, starting toward the door. "I'm sure we can track it down." As they left, he glanced back. Bob already had the magnifying goggles down over his eyes and was bending over his model.

Joe parked the van around the curve from Mike's house, and he and Frank went the rest of the way on foot. No one seemed to notice as they walked up Mike's driveway, circled the garage, and vaulted the low hurricane fence that separated the backyard from the woods.

"Do you see anything that looks like a path?" Joe asked.

"Someone's been here lately," Frank said, pointing to a footprint in a muddy patch, where the ground had thawed a little that day. "Come on."

Once they were in the woods the path became easier to follow. Joe took the lead. "We must be nearly there," he said, peeking back over his shoulder. Suddenly his foot caught on something, and he started to fall.

At that moment Frank heard a whining sound overhead. He turned and saw a tree at least a foot thick and eight feet tall toppling over. Joe was directly beneath it!

Chapter

12

"JOE, LOOK OUT!" Frank shouted. He lunged forward, tackled Joe around the waist, and pulled him back toward him. He fell into a pile of brown leaves with Joe on top of him. An instant later the tree crashed across the path, only inches from Joe's left foot.

Joe scrambled up, then turned to give Frank a hand. "Are you okay?" he demanded.

"I've got a couple of dents in my back that weren't there before," Frank replied. "But they're not bad. How about you?"

"I'm fine. That tree is dead. It must have been leaning against some branches, poised to fall, and something or somebody—" Suddenly Joe held up his hand for silence.

Frank listened, too. Someone, not too far away, was moving quietly away from them.

Frank gestured with his head, and he and Joe started to follow quickly and silently.

Frank thought they were beginning to gain on whoever was ahead of them. Then his foot came down on a fallen branch hidden by leaves. It broke with a loud *crack.* A moment later there was the sound of many branches snapping around a bend in the path ahead. Frank broke into a run, with Joe right behind him. He reached the bend just in time to see someone bent over the handlebars of a mountain bike speed around a bend in the path. Frank stopped running—he knew he and Joe had lost the race.

Only a tire mark in the mud showed that the mountain bike had been past.

"Did that guy remind you of anybody?" Frank asked.

"Mike, definitely," Joe replied. "I'm ninety-five percent sure."

"Me, too," Frank said. "Let's go back and hunt for that shack. It's pretty obvious that he's been hiding there. Maybe he left in such a hurry that we'll find some clues."

"I want to check that fallen tree, too," Joe replied. "Nobody can tell me it just happened to fall over when I walked past."

They stopped at the base of the tree, and Frank stooped down and felt around before straightening up with an inch-thick forked stick in his hand.

"Just as I thought," he said. He pointed to the tree. "See this scrape mark near the bottom? Mike must have propped up the tree with this stick. Then he strung wire across the path, fastened it to the bottom of the stick, and covered the wire with leaves. When you tripped on it, you pulled the stick out from under the trunk and the tree fell."

Joe studied the ground on the opposite side of the path, then picked up a coiled wire. "You're right," he announced. "He even used brown wire, to make it harder to see. I wouldn't mind having a little private conversation with Mike," he added.

"First, let's see what we can find in the way of evidence," Frank replied. He led the way to the thicket Bob had described and began to circle it. On the far side from the path was a low, narrow tunnel through the bushes. Protecting his face with his bent arm, Frank pushed past the branches and found himself in a small clearing, facing a low, rough shack. One pane of glass was missing from the two small windows, and the opening was stuffed with rags.

Frank opened the rotting plank door and stepped inside. On a crude shelf under one of the windows were several cans of tuna, a box of crackers, and three bottles of diet cola. An air mattress, partly deflated, lay on the floor against the far wall, with a faded khaki sleeping bag spread out on it. In the corner behind it was an old Boy Scout knapsack. Frank picked it up and read out loud the markings on the flap: "Mike T.-Eagle Pat.-Tr fifty-five."

From behind him, Joe said, "Huh. Either we're dealing with somebody named Pat Eagle, or that really was Mike who just rode away on that bike. Who else could it be?"

Joe's voice changed. "Frank—look at this." He held out a sheet of grimy typing paper. Frank read,

for 2000 A Week in small BILLS I keep My mouth shut put money in Bay Monday or else

In classic style, the words had been clipped from a newspaper and pasted on the sheet. Frank suspected that the word *BILLS* had come from a headline about a pro football game.

"Where did you find this?" Frank asked.

"It was in among these other sheets of paper," Joe said. "But they're all blank. You realize what this means? Mike is no crusading journalist hiding out from powerful interests. He's just a crummy blackmailer who's afraid his victim will catch up with him. Now I guess we know where he got the money for that new computer, the creep!"

"Hold on," Frank warned. "If Mike's a blackmailer, why is the note still here? Why didn't he give it to the target? For all we know, he pasted it up for a joke or just as a way to pass the time while he was hiding out. But if he did, he got rid of the scissors, paste, and old newspapers. None of that's here."

Joe held the blackmail note up to the window, then did the same with one of the other sheets of paper in his hand.

"These sheets all have the same watermark," he announced. "But the note is on a much cheaper grade of paper. The only mark on it looks like an oil stain. Maybe I *was* jumping to conclusions, just a little bit. What if Mike *found* this note, as part of his investigation?"

Frank scratched his head. "Could be. But why leave money in the bay? Can't you just see somebody going out in a rowboat and tying a plastic bag full of tens and twenties to one of the buoys?"

"Wait a minute!" Joe exclaimed. "Tens and twenties—that's what the Project Planet Earth money was, and it was *Monday* that it turned up missing. Maybe the blackmail victim stole it to make the payoff, and that's how it ended up in Mike's desk. So he *is* the blackmailer, after all!"

"But we decided that Mike wouldn't leave that money in an unlocked drawer, that somebody put it there to frame him for the theft," Frank pointed out.

"Oh. Right." Joe made an exasperated noise and tucked the blackmail note between two other sheets of paper to protect it.

"You know," Frank continued, "the only way we're going to sort all this out is by getting some answers from Mike. And to do that, we're going to have to find him. Maybe he's gone back to his house. I can't imagine that he'll be able to stay away from that new computer of his for much longer."

They followed the path back to Mike's yard, slipped around to the front, and rang the bell. After a short silence Frank heard faint footsteps approaching the door, which stayed solidly shut. Frank rang again. He had an eerie sense that someone was watching him, and when he looked at the peephole, he recalled that some light had been coming through it before. Now it was dark. Someone *was* watching him. Mike? His mother? It didn't seem to matter very much. Whoever it was obviously did not mean to answer the door.

"Come on, we'll try another time," Frank told Joe loudly.

As they walked down the driveway, Frank noticed one set of muddy tire tracks left by a mountain bike.

Back at the van, Joe said, "Why don't we wait here a little while, just in case Mike decides to take a ride?"

"Okay with me," Frank replied. "We can use the time to talk over the case. If it is just one case, that is. Sometimes I have the feeling it's three or four different cases that are all mixed up."

Joe said, "What are the questions we need to answer? First, who is trying to sabotage Project Planet Earth? Second, who took the money and hid it in Mike's desk? Third, what was Mike doing at the UniPlast plant on Monday evening? Fourth, what is this big story Mike's been working on? And fifth, who is blackmailing whom, and about what? That about covers it, I think."

"You forgot one important question," Frank said. "Sixth—how did Vic Krieger die?"

Joe stared at him. "But we know the answer to that one," he said. "Krieger fell into the baling machine."

"While it was on—after hours?" Frank replied. "Somehow I can't see it, no matter what the police think. I know it *could* have happened like that, but it's just too much for me to buy."

Joe's eyes widened. "You mean, you think Mike . . ." His voice trailed off.

"I didn't say I had an answer," Frank said. "I said I had another question. But we do have a pretty obvious answer to your first question, about the sabotage. Lucy Velez. She'd love to see Erika's campaign fall flat. Twice, somebody who looked an awful lot like her has attacked us in a Planet Earth van. And if that's not enough, she and her team are the clear favorites to win that ski trip. I say it's time we asked her a few more questions."

"So do I," Joe replied. "Do you have her address?"

Frank whipped out the Bayport phone book they kept in the van and gave the address to Joe. The Velez house was east of downtown Bayport, a couple of blocks from Memorial Park. The first part of the drive seemed to take forever. Traffic was barely moving. As the Hardys approached the interstate entrance, Frank saw that the traffic light at the intersection was dark. A police officer in a brilliant orange raincoat was blowing his whistle and waving his arms. He was obviously doing his best to sort out the confusion.

Once past the bottleneck, they started to roll. Soon Memorial Park appeared on their left. Joe was slowing down for the turn onto Lucy's street when a light blue compact car rolled past a stop sign and darted in front of him. Joe hit the brakes, then exclaimed, "Frank! Wasn't that Lucy?"

Frank replayed the fleeting glimpse he had had of the person at the wheel of the blue car. "Yeah, I think so," he said.

Joe turned around in a driveway and started in the direction the blue car had taken. It was still in sight, four blocks ahead.

Gnet-gnet. Gnet-gnet. Frank reached for the cellular phone.

"Hello?" he said.

"Frank, it's Callie," he heard. "Listen, I'm calling from a pay phone. You've got to get over here right away. I'm on the trail of the person who's passing out those fake leaflets."

"Great!" Frank exclaimed. "This is the break we needed. Where are you?"

Callie named an intersection not far from the Bayport High School stadium. Frank passed the information on to Joe, who turned right to start across town.

"We'll be there in ten or fifteen minutes," Frank started to say, but Callie interrupted him.

"Frank, there she is," she blurted out, her voice rising with excitement. "She just turned onto this block. She's passing by in one of the green project vans, not twenty feet away."

"Who is it?" Frank demanded. "Did you recognize her?"

"Of course I did," Callie replied, with surprise in her voice. "I thought you already knew. It's Lucy Velez!"

Chapter

13

MOMENTS LATER the Hardys were racing across town in the twilight to join Callie. Joe slowed for a moment, to pass a double-parked delivery truck, then sped up again. "I'm *sure* that was Lucy we saw in the blue car," he insisted.

"I didn't get a very good look," Frank admitted. "But I thought it was her, too. So unless she's developed the ability to be in two places at once—"

"Somebody is going around disguised as her," Joe said, finishing the sentence. "And trying to put the blame on her for sabotaging Project Planet Earth. Unless the girl we saw wasn't really Lucy, but somebody disguised as her, to give her an alibi."

"That doesn't hold up," Frank said. "Nobody

could have known that we'd be at that corner right then. On the other hand, it's been suspiciously easy to get glimpses of the girl who tried to run us down. It was almost as if she *wanted* to give people a chance to notice her sunglasses and black ponytail."

Frank reached for the telephone. "We'd better check some of our facts before we start working on conclusions," he said, dialing.

"Hello, Mrs. Velez? This is Frank Hardy. Is Lucy in? Oh, I see. All right, thanks. Oh—what kind of car is she driving? I'm going to the mall myself. Maybe I'll spot her there."

Frank switched off the handset and turned to Joe. "We just missed Lucy," he reported. "She left home a few minutes ago to run a couple of errands. And she's driving a light blue compact."

"All right!" Joe exclaimed. "Now we're getting somewhere!"

Joe made a left turn. Two more minutes brought them to a block dominated by a home improvement center. Joe spotted Callie's car in the parking lot. As he pulled into the slot next to it, Callie jumped out and hurried over. Frank reached back to open the rear door for her.

"She just went by again, not a minute ago!" Callie exclaimed, climbing inside. "I wanted to follow her, but I figured I'd better wait for you."

"Which way?" Joe demanded, already backing out of the parking space.

Callie gestured, and Joe took off. Traffic was

lighter now, and he was able to make good time, but after five minutes he had practically no hope of spotting the green van. It could have turned off at any one of a dozen intersections.

"Oh, can't we try just a little longer?" Callie pleaded. "You never know. I already saw Lucy twice. She might still be driving around in the neighborhood."

"Maybe," Frank said. "But it's looking pretty certain that that wasn't Lucy Velez you saw. It was someone impersonating her."

While Callie listened openmouthed, Joe and Frank told her about seeing the real Lucy just a few minutes before, across town.

"But I *saw* her," Callie insisted.

"Did you see her face?" Frank asked. "Or was it mainly the hair and glasses that you noticed?"

"Well— Okay, I get the point," Callie replied. "I guess I couldn't swear it was Lucy. But why—"

"This isn't the only try at framing somebody," Joe pointed out. "There was that missing money that was planted in Mike Tano's desk, too. What do Mike and Lucy have in common?"

"They're both on the key list for the student government office," Frank recalled. "But I don't think that's what you're getting at."

Joe grinned. "You're right, it isn't. No, both of them, at that first meeting, had doubts or questions about Project Planet Earth, or at least about Erika's version of it. Now, suppose somebody has a secret reason to wreck the project, but doesn't want to take any chance of being found out. Wouldn't it make sense to leave evidence pointing to a couple of people who are on record as being sort of against the project?"

"That makes sense," Callie said. "But why would anybody want to wreck the project?"

"That's a good question," Frank said. "And here's another that just occurred to me. Why have they done such a bad job of it? The missing money was found almost immediately. The phony leaflets have been a nuisance, but they haven't been distributed to everyone, just a few houses got them. In fact, on the whole, Project Planet Earth seems like it's going to be a big success."

Joe pulled over to the curb and turned to face Frank and Callie. "I just thought of an answer," he announced. "What if the person we're talking about doesn't really want to wreck the project, but does want to make everybody *think* that somebody's trying to wreck the project?"

Callie was skeptical. "Why would somebody do that?"

"I don't know," Joe said with a shrug. "To get more publicity for what we're doing, maybe?"

Frank shook his head. "If that's the reason, whoever it is must be pretty disappointed. Erika did a good job of keeping the missing money quiet, and no one's said much about the counterfeit leaflets, either. No, I'm coming around more and more to the idea that Mike's big story is somehow the key to the mystery. But as long as he keeps out of sight, I don't see how we can get far in solving it."

"We'd better get home. It's getting dark and I can hardly see," Joe said, pulling out into the traffic lane. He didn't bother trying to hide the discouragement he felt. "We still have a team meeting to go to."

As he drove, he thought about what Frank had said. Had they really come to a dead end, just when it seemed that the case was breaking wide open?

"You know," he said suddenly, "even if Mike's story is the key, we don't have to sit around waiting for him to share it with us. Anyone who investigates something leaves traces. What if we can find out who he's been talking to and what kind of questions he's been asking? That should give us a pretty clear idea of what he's after."

"The phone log!" Callie exclaimed. "Remember? It's a new regulation this semester. Any student organization that has a telephone in its office has to keep a complete log of calls. It's supposed to help keep costs down."

"Hey, that's right," Frank said eagerly. "The log in the *Review* office will give us the names and numbers of everyone Mike called—or at least, everyone he called from there. We'll go by during our first free period tomorrow morning."

*   *   *

The door to the *Review* office was open. Several students were hurrying around the office, and Frank guessed they were on some kind of deadline. Valerie Shoemaker was standing at the big table in the middle of the room, with a pair of long scissors in one hand and a rectangular piece of paper in the other. The table was covered with large and small bits of paper. She glanced at Joe and Frank as they walked in.

"Would you believe this?" she demanded, gesturing toward the table. "With a desktop publishing program we could lay out the paper in one-tenth the time and do a neater job for less money. But our computer isn't powerful enough to run one. So it's scissors and tape for us. Grrr!"

"No word yet from Mike?" asked Frank.

"Nothing," Valerie replied. "I can't believe he really means for us to put out next week's issue on our own. Up until now, he's done all the really important stuff himself. What if we mess up?"

"I have a hunch you're doing fine," Frank said. "Listen, is the phone log around? Maybe we can find Mike by checking with people he's been calling."

"On his desk, next to the phone," Valerie said absently. She had already returned to staring at the layout sheets.

Frank and Joe scanned the phone log together. Most of Mike's calls during the previous two weeks had been either to manufacturing companies or to firms that specialized in waste disposal. There were also a few calls made to state and local environmental protection offices.

Joe sighed, disappointed. "He was obviously working on some kind of environmental story to tie in with Project Planet Earth. Big deal."

"He told people it was an important story that would blow the town wide open," Frank pointed out. "That doesn't sound like a simple let's-all-help-save-the-planet piece. I'd like to know what he wanted from all these people he called."

" 'When you want to know something, ask,' " Joe said, quoting their father. " 'Somebody just might tell you.' " He reached for the telephone.

"Who are you calling?" Frank asked.

Joe pointed to the name of one of the waste disposal firms. "He called them three times," he explained with his palm over the microphone. Then, into the phone, he said, "Oh, hello, this is the Bayport High *Review*. We'd like to double-check some of the facts you gave us before we go to press. . . . Yes, that's right. . . . Oh, I see. . . . Yes, we'll do that. . . . Thanks very much."

Joe hung up and gave Frank a victorious grin. "The company specializes in carting away toxic wastes. Mike called them to get figures on how much of the stuff different companies in Bayport get rid of every year. The woman I spoke to told me I'd have to check with the companies themselves. Apparently some of them use more than one disposal firm."

"Why?" Frank asked. "Wouldn't that just complicate everything for them?"

"No idea," Joe replied. "Unless they've got some reason for wanting things complicated."

"Let me see that phone log again," Frank said. He reached into his pocket for his notebook and thumbed through it until he found the page he was looking for, then compared it to the log. He was reaching for the telephone when it rang. After a glance at the other staff members who were obviously too busy to be bothered, he picked it up.

"Bayport High *Review*, good morning," he said.

"Listen, snooper, and listen good," someone said in a throaty whisper. "Mind your own business and keep your mouth shut, or we're gonna shut it for you—permanently."

Chapter

14

Outside in the corridor, the bell rang. Frank pressed the receiver closer to his ear and covered his other ear with his palm to block out the noise. The sound of the bell came through, anyway. Then he heard a quiet click, and the line went dead.

In a few words he told Joe about the call.

"Could you tell if it was a man or woman?" Joe asked.

"Afraid not," Frank said.

"How did whoever it was know we were here?" Joe continued. "Or—wait a minute—maybe the call wasn't meant for us. All you said was 'Bayport High *Review*.' Maybe the caller thought you were Mike."

Frank looked over his shoulder. "Valerie?" he called. He had to repeat himself twice before she heard. "Have you been getting any peculiar calls here?"

Valerie stared at him blankly for a moment, then said, "Oh, was that the whisperer? I wish Mike would come back so he could answer his crank calls himself. It gives me the creepy-crawlies."

Under prodding from Joe, she added that she had answered three or four of the calls over the previous two days. "All pretty much the same— 'Tell Mike to keep his mouth shut, or we'll shut it for him,'" she said. "I guess newspapers get sicko stuff like that all the time, but I wish whoever it is would take his own advice and shut up."

A moment later she was completely engrossed in her work again.

"All right," Joe said. "So it *was* aimed at Mike. Maybe he has good reasons to stay out of sight, after all. Hey, didn't I hear the bell a few minutes ago? We seem to be cutting class."

"The bell!" Frank said, grabbing Joe's arm. "Wait a minute—I heard the bell with both ears!"

"Sure you did," Joe replied. "So what?"

"Don't you see? I had the telephone pressed to one ear, and I heard the bell, anyway. The sound was coming over the phone. And that means that the whisperer was calling from a telephone right here in school! Not only that, when the caller hung up I didn't hear a ding, the way you usually do when somebody calls you from a pay phone."

"Hey, keep it down, will you?" Valerie called. "I'm trying to work."

Frank pulled Joe into the corner and said softly, "We've got to find out what Mike's story is about. Chances are, he worked on it here at the office as well as at home. I'm going to try to locate it on the computer. If Valerie notices, distract her somehow."

The computer was already booted. Frank called up a directory of the hard disk and spotted a subdirectory called MIKETANO, but when he tried to get into it he discovered that Mike had used a password on this one, too. He tried one combination of letters after another, but none of them worked. He was about to give up when he noticed an old engraving taped to the wall behind the monitor. The legend read, Pioneer Journalist Joseph Pulitzer 1847–1911. Frank counted the letters in *Pulitzer*, then typed them in and hit the Enter key.

The screen changed to display Mike's subdirectory. "Modest guy," Frank muttered to himself.

The subdirectory was loaded with file names. Frank ran his finger down the list, leaving a line in the dust that had collected on the monitor screen. Finally he saw it: UNIPLAST. According to the directory, the file had last been modified just before Mike disappeared.

Holding his breath, Frank called up the file.

A long jumble of notes and figures appeared on the screen. The longer Frank looked through them, the clearer the picture became. Given the level of production at UniPlast and the manufacturing processes they were known to be using, the factory had to generate at least three times as much toxic waste every year as it was known to be disposing of legally. Where was the rest going?

An image came into Frank's mind of the metal drums, supposedly containing packing pellets, that were too heavy to be moved by hand. Was that how UniPlast was smuggling the excess waste out of the factory? There was no way a drum containing only packing pellets could be so heavy.

He found the right place in his notebook again and dialed the telephone.

"Yeah, RJ," a gruff voice answered.

"Hi, this is the *Review,* the Bayport High School newspaper," Frank said. "We're running a story in next week's issue about illegal dumping of toxic waste. We thought you should know that your company is mentioned in it, along with UniPlast."

"What!" the voice exclaimed. "Listen, who is this?"

"The Bayport High *Review,*" Frank repeated. "Do you have any comment about charges that your firm is engaged in illegal dumping?"

If he did, it was drowned out by the sound of the telephone being slammed down.

"That should stir things up a little," Frank murmured, smiling to himself.

"What was that about?" Joe demanded.

Frank showed him Mike's notes and explained what he thought they meant. Then he stood up and said, "We're going to pay another little visit to UniPlast."

Joe gave him a surprised look but followed him out of the room without argument. Valerie didn't glance up, even when Joe called, "See you."

On the way to the school parking lot, Joe said, "We were barred from that place just yesterday. Remember?"

"Uh-huh," Frank replied. "But we'll be arriving there during lunch hour. If the relief man's on the gate, he may not know about us. Anyway, we have to go there. We've got a whole load of questions, and that's where the answers are."

While driving to the plant, Frank gave Joe some more details of what he had learned from Mike's computer file.

"Wow!" Joe exclaimed. "You mean the main sponsor of Project Planet Earth is also a major polluter? I know someone who's going to have egg on her face once this comes out."

That thought had occurred to Frank, too. "I wonder," he said slowly. "Just how far do you think Erika might go to keep this from coming out?"

Joe didn't answer. He was slowing down for

the turn into the UniPlast entrance. The gate stood open, but as the van swung in an older man in uniform stepped out of the watchman's cabin and motioned for him to stop.

"Can I help you?" he asked.

Joe had a Project Planet Earth badge ready in his hand. He showed the watchman the badge and said, "Erika Rodoski, the head of our project, sent us with a message for Mr. Stone. He's expecting us."

The man nodded. "Go on in," he said. "Guest parking is around to the left."

As the van began to roll again, Frank glanced back and saw the watchman picking up the telephone in the cabin. "Our arrival is being announced," he said. "What if he had called first before letting us in?"

Joe grinned. "I would have been indignant with Erika for not telling them we were coming," he said. "A little indignation can do wonders."

A canteen truck was sitting in the middle of the parking lot, surrounded by people in work clothes and heavy jackets eating sandwiches. Joe found a vacant spot near the loading dock and parked the van facing out. "We may have to leave in a hurry," he explained.

As they walked up the ramp, Frank said out of the side of his mouth, "The motto of the day is Look like you belong."

Inside the loading bay, Frank and Joe stepped to one side to let a young guy pushing a hand truck go by. He stared at them curiously but didn't say anything. Frank noticed that there was a new set of perhaps a dozen drums of packing pellets waiting to be shipped out. As he walked past them, he deliberately stumbled and caught himself on one of them. It was so heavy it didn't budge the slightest bit.

He and Joe had passed through the door to the recycling machines and into a corridor to the right when Frank was struck by an idea. He stopped so suddenly that Joe bumped into him.

"What is it?" Joe asked in a low voice.

"That blackmail note," Frank replied, just as quietly. "What if 'bay' meant the loading bay? Mike could have found the note right here."

"We'll ask him the next time we see him," Joe said grimly.

After twenty feet or so, the hallway came to a *T*. From the left came the noise and smells of the plastic recycling operation. From the right, Frank heard a computer printer and a ringing telephone. He chose the right, and Joe followed.

After a few steps, Frank saw that one wall of the hall was replaced by a large window that extended from waist height nearly to the ceiling. Frank glanced into each office as they passed. The first two were empty. In the third, a woman talking on the phone glanced up and met Frank's gaze. For a moment she seemed puzzled. Then she swiveled around with her back to the Hardys and went on with her conversation.

The fourth room contained rows of file cabinets. A few of the drawers were not quite shut, as if someone had consulted them and then been called away in a hurry. Frank wished he could go in and search for a file on RJ Transports, but the wide window onto the hallway made discovery practically certain. In any case, he was not sure that he would know how to interpret any evidence he might find there.

As they approached the end of the hall, Frank held up one hand to caution Joe. The last door on the left stood open. From beyond it came the sound of angry shouting.

"Story in some two-bit high school paper! I said I'd handle the situation, and I will. You just sit tight, Ralph, and we'll come out of this smelling like roses."

Frank recognized Sol Stone's voice and realized that he must be on the telephone. Could Ralph be the *R* in RJ Transports?

"Okay, Ralph," Stone continued. "You calm down, take your heart medicine, and I'll take care of everything. Of course I'm sure. Listen, I've got a call on the other line. I'll get back to you in a couple of minutes."

After a brief silence, Stone said, "An appointment? With me? No, I don't know anything about that. I'll check on it. No, no, Leon, it's okay. But don't let anybody else past the gate unless you know who they are and what they're doing here."

Stone was silent for a minute, and then Frank heard him say, "Erika? Listen, did you send two kids from your school over here to meet with me about something? I have no idea what their names are. They told my man at the gate that they came from you. Yeah? That's what I was afraid of."

Frank motioned to Joe to start backing down the corridor, as Stone shouted, "Andersen—tell the guards to fan out and search the plant. A couple of those high school kids sneaked onto the premises. I want them out, now. And tell the guards I don't care if they get roughed up a little in the process."

Frank glanced over at Joe and motioned behind them with his head. Then he began to tiptoe backward. He was edging past one of the office doors when he sensed its being opened behind him.

"Hey!" someone cried.

As Frank started to recoil, he felt a hand clamp down over his mouth.

Chapter

15

OUT OF THE CORNER of his eye, Joe saw someone reach out to grab Frank. He whirled around
and drew back his arm to throw a punch. Then
he stopped himself, recognizing the pale,
strained face of Mike Tano.

"Quick—you've got to help me get away,"
Mike whispered urgently. He let go of Frank.
"I've got photocopies of all the evidence inside
my shirt. Stone will do anything to keep it from
coming out—*anything!*"

Joe wanted to ask Mike, evidence of what? But
this wasn't the moment. He glanced around to be
sure of his bearings, then said, "Okay, follow me."
Joe led the way down the corridor past the win-
dowed offices as Frank and Mike followed. They
were nearing the side corridor that led to the loading bay when Joe heard a shout from behind him.

"There they are. Stop them!"

Joe glanced back over his shoulder. Two guards were running down the hall toward them, their clubs drawn and ready. Stone was right behind them.

"Run for it!" Joe called to Mike and Frank. He started to follow his own advice. A moment later the door ahead of him crashed open. Two more guards appeared, blocking their escape.

Joe ran toward them, and the guards raised their clubs to chest height. Joe scanned the hallway and tried to sort through his options. It didn't take long, because he didn't have many. Practically none, in fact. Then he noticed a group of pipes that crossed the hallway a foot below the ceiling. The guards were waiting for them about a yard beyond that point. Perfect!

As he approached the crucial spot, Joe crouched slightly and put all his force into a leap upward. Wrapping his hands around the pipes, he swung forward and kicked out, hard, with both feet. His left foot connected solidly, catching one of the guards just below the ribs. The guard gave a loud grunt and fell backward.

Joe wasn't so lucky with his right foot. The other guard saw it coming, dodged to the side, and managed to land a blow on Joe's thigh with his club. Joe released the pipes and dropped to the floor. He landed on both feet, but his right leg wasn't obeying orders. It crumpled under him. As he fell sideways, he saw the second guard raising his club for another blow, this one aimed at his head.

Joe clasped his bent arms around his head and started to roll away. Just then Joe saw Frank launch himself in a flying tackle at the second guard.

"Come on, come on, they'll catch us!" Mike was holding open the door to the loading bay, jumping from one foot to the other with excitement and dread. Joe scrambled to his feet and gave Frank a quick hand, then dashed through the doorway. A glance back showed that the other two guards, red with anger, were less than a dozen feet away.

Joe gave the swinging door a shove, slamming it in their faces. That gained a few seconds, but he knew it wouldn't be enough for the three of them to reach the van and get away. Then he saw the forklift sitting there. The key was in the lock. He vaulted into the operator's seat and shouted, "Onto the back." As Frank and Mike jumped on, he turned the key, spun the wheel to the right, and put the pedal to the metal.

It took just moments to realize that the battery-powered vehicle had not been built for drag racing. They were less than halfway across the loading bay when the guards came bursting through the door and formed a line in front of them. But if the forklift wasn't very fast, it was forceful. Joe managed to raise the fork to about waist height. Then he aimed the machine straight at the line of guards. They held out until he was a few feet away, then scattered. As the forklift lumbered past, one of the guards tried to jump on. Frank's solid left to the jaw changed his plans.

Moments later Joe brought the forklift to a stop next to the van, and he, Frank, and Mike piled in. Joe laid a track of rubber on the concrete as he started for the exit. The watchman was just starting to swing the gate closed, but when he saw the van speeding toward him he jumped aside, leaving a wide enough gap for their escape.

"Whew!" Frank said, grabbing the cellular phone. "Nothing like a little excitement to liven up your day!"

"Who are you calling?" Mike asked, leaning forward between the two front bucket seats.

"The Bayport Police Department," Frank replied.

"No! You can't!" Mike lunged for the phone.

"Why not?" Frank asked, holding him off.

"They—I'm afraid they'll think I'm a murderer," Mike admitted. "And I don't know how to prove I'm not."

It took a lot of probing from Frank and Joe, but eventually Mike explained that on Monday evening he had managed to sneak into the Uni-Plast factory. After half an hour of dodging a uniformed guard, he had found a hiding place behind some drums and decided to wait until later to explore.

"But while I was crouching there in the

dark," Mike continued, "I heard two guys arguing in the next room. Then a machine started up, and one of them screamed. It was horrible. I heard the other one run away, so I went to look. I wish I hadn't."

Frank turned in his seat and stared at Mike. "You heard an argument just before Krieger was killed?" he exclaimed. "That makes you a crucial witness! Who was he arguing with? Over what?"

Mike hesitated. "I'm not positive, but I think the guy who was killed was trying to blackmail the other guy. And I suspect I know who the other guy was, too. But I'm not sure enough to accuse him, even now."

"Blackmail?" Joe said. "You mean that note we found in your shack? Where did you get it?"

"I found it on the floor when I was hiding," Mike responded. "I stuck it in my pocket, without even remembering about fingerprints and all. Then I sneaked out of the factory and ran away to hide in the woods. That was when I realized that I'd left my flashlight behind."

"We found it," Joe told him. "We went to the plant looking for clues after your mom asked us to investigate. Then she told us to quit. What happened there?"

"I called her when I went into hiding and asked her to make sure no one was looking for me," Mike said. "I was terrified of being implicated in Krieger's death."

"The police think Krieger's death was an accident, but your version makes it sound an awful lot like murder," Frank said. "You'll have to tell the police, you know, and the sooner the better." He reached for the phone again. This time, Mike didn't try to stop him.

Half an hour later Frank, Joe, and Mike returned to the UniPlast plant in the company of Detective Broussard, Officer Con Riley, and two other uniformed officers.

Frank led the way to Sol Stone's office. The door was closed. When Broussard knocked, Stone himself opened it. Over his shoulder, Frank saw Erika Rodoski standing next to his desk. When she saw the police and recognized Frank, she turned so pale that Frank thought she was going to faint.

"What's the trouble, Officer?" Stone demanded. "Aren't those the kids I've had to kick off the premises a couple of times?"

Broussard said, "Some serious allegations have been brought to our attention, sir. We have to check them out. You understand."

Frank thought that Stone understood all too well. He retreated behind his desk, sat down, and said, "What sort of allegations?"

Mike pushed forward and leaned over Stone's desk. "I found documents in your files that prove your company's been illegally dumping tons of poisonous waste," he burst out. "And I overheard your argument with that guy who was

146

killed. I recognize your voice. You killed him, didn't you!"

The only sign that Stone had heard was that he stopped blinking for almost a minute. Then he looked back at Broussard and said, "Taking confidential records from a company's files is larceny, isn't it? I assure you I intend to bring charges. And while you have him under lock and key, you'll want to look into his tale of being on the premises after hours the other night. I don't intend to make reckless charges, but I will point out that Vic Krieger's job was to protect this company against just such intrusions. It was a job that could turn dangerous at any moment. Apparently it did, on Monday night."

Frank saw Broussard giving Mike a doubtful glance and decided it was time to step in. "Erika?" he said. "When did you find out that UniPlast is engaged in illegal dumping?"

She stared at him. "Why—never! That's crazy! What are you talking about?"

"It's the only explanation for all the mischief you've been up to," Frank continued. "Starting with that fake blood in the box for the drawing. Nobody else knew what that coffee can was for. And then pretending to wreck Project Planet Earth while disguising yourself as Lucy Velez. Pretending the money from the first week's collection had been stolen, then trying to frame Mike for the theft."

"What!" Mike exclaimed. "Erika, you did that? I thought we were friends!"

She gave him a pleading look, then turned her gaze back to Frank.

"I have to admire your nerve," he said. "When we looked closely at the theft of the money, it seemed impossible. How could anyone have taken the money from your locked desk, substituted a folded newspaper that was only then being put on the stands, and slipped the money into Mike's desk, all in a short time? Then I remembered. Monday afternoon, while Joe and I were standing in the hall, you showed up at the *Review* office with a big envelope and went inside. You were alone in there for a couple of minutes—plenty long enough to plant the money. No one else could have done it, but you could, easily."

Erika gulped in a breath, then cried, "Okay, okay! But don't you see? I didn't know at first that Mr. Stone was supporting our project to keep everybody from suspecting his company was a big polluter. I figured it out right after the project members had voted to adopt my plan. Mr. Stone let me look through some of his files so I could get information about the plant for the leaflets, and I accidentally came across the files on the toxic waste disposal."

"Why didn't you report UniPlast then?" Joe asked.

Erika sighed. "I was trying to protect the project. I overheard Mike on the phone in the

148

Review office when I was dropping off a press release, and I knew he was close to breaking the pollution thing. Once he printed the story, Project Planet Earth would be dead. I couldn't let that happen. The project was too important. If it failed, it would set back the cause of recycling for years! So I faked the theft and tried to make it look like he was responsible. I wasn't going to let him be arrested or anything like that. I just wanted to make sure that nobody would pay attention to what he wrote."

"For a journalist, that's worse than murder," Mike told her.

"Why did you try to run us down, dressed up like Lucy?" Joe demanded. "Not to mention trying to force us off the viaduct. That *was* you, wasn't it?"

"I wasn't trying to hurt you," Erika insisted. "When I saw you looking at that leaflet I'd just been posting, I got spooked. I knew that with the Hardys on my trail, it was just a matter of time before I was caught. And the next day, after I planted the money, I followed you. When I realized you were on your way to Mike's house, I had to do something to stop you. But I never meant to hurt you. I wanted to *help* people, to save the environment."

"But why the disguise?" Frank asked. "Why try to pin what you were doing on Lucy Velez?"

"I want to be president of the student body next year," Erika said simply. "I'm the best for the job, and I deserve to be elected. But I knew that Lucy would try to stop me. She always does. Look at the way she tried to keep me from heading up Project Planet Earth. So I decided to stop her first, by making it look like she was wrecking a campaign that everyone else in school supported."

"Lies and dirty tricks," Joe said. "That's not much of a recipe for good student government."

"It is if it works," Erika snapped, glaring at him.

"Let's get back to Krieger's death," Detective Broussard said. "Mr. Stone, were you here on the premises on Monday evening?"

"Why—no," Stone replied. "I left about six. After dinner at the country club, I took a long drive. I often do that. I find it soothes my nerves."

"And you drive a red foreign sedan, license plate UNIPLAST, is that right?" Broussard continued.

"Everybody knows that," Stone said with a short laugh.

Con Riley took a paper from his pocket. "Mr. Stone, at eight forty-seven P.M. on Monday, one of our patrol cars responded to a report of a prowler near your factory. I wouldn't be surprised if it was this young man that the report concerned. They didn't find the prowler, but they did notice a red car with your license plate on it parked at the side of the plant. Any comment?"

"Yes. This whole thing is ridiculous!" Stone

declared. "I may have stopped by to pick up some papers I needed. I don't recall."

Frank produced a photocopy of the blackmail note. "A paper such as this one?" he asked quietly. "When the police take a closer look at Krieger's home, do you think they'll find the materials Krieger used to make it? Or even records he saved, to make his hold over you stronger?"

This time Stone blinked. Twice. Then he said, in a calm, emotionless voice, "I didn't kill him. It was an accident, just as the police thought from the first."

"Hold it, please," Detective Broussard said. He took a small card from his jacket pocket and read Stone a list of his rights. "Do you understand?" he concluded.

Stone waved his hand. "Of course I do," he replied. "And I didn't kill him. It's true, he thought he had uncovered some embarrassing facts about UniPlast, and he tried to make money from them. When I refused to pay blackmail, he attacked me. I pushed him away, he got tangled in the baler's conveyor belt, and—well, you know the rest."

"How did the machine happen to be operating?" Frank asked.

Stone gave him a look of hatred. "I'm not going to answer any more questions until I talk to my lawyer," he announced. His voice suddenly rose to a scream. "And get those snoopy kids off my property—*now!*"

*   *   *

"Get your spicy hot organic apple cider, right here," Vanessa called out. "It's good for you and the environment, too."

Next to her, Joe was kept busy drawing cups of cider from the converted coffee urn and handing them to customers. The buzz of a happy crowd filled the school auditorium.

"Two ciders, buddy, and step on it," somebody growled. Joe looked up quickly and found Frank and Callie grinning at him.

"Hey, who's minding the bake sale stand?" Joe asked, as he poured the ciders.

"Valerie Shoemaker took over," Callie explained. "Would you believe that people bought all of my granola muffins in the first fifteen minutes? Chet bought two of them."

"The carnival is a real success," Vanessa said. "I'm glad. I was afraid all that bad business with Erika and UniPlast would spoil it."

Chet and Biff drifted over, just as Mike hurried up from the other direction.

"Have you heard the latest?" Mike demanded. "I just got off the phone with Detective Broussard, and Sol Stone has agreed to plead guilty to a murder charge. Plus, it looks like UniPlast is going to have to pay huge fines for their illegal dumping."

"Great!" Callie said. "Hey, Mike, I heard your story about UniPlast is going to run in one of the big New York newspapers. Is that true?"

Mike turned bright red and looked down at his toes. "Er—yes, it is," he mumbled.

Joe reached over and slapped him on the back. "Way to go, guy!" he exclaimed.

As the others added their congratulations, Lucy Velez came over. "What are we celebrating?" she asked.

Callie explained. Lucy leaned over and gave Mike a big kiss on the cheek. His face turned even redder.

"We should congratulate you, too, Lucy," Chet said. "It looks like your team will be going on that ski trip. I heard the mayor said he's going to make sure that UmPlast keeps all its promises to the project."

"Thanks, Chet," Lucy replied. "It's too bad every team can't go to Vermont. Everybody has worked really hard to make this project a success."

"That reminds me—I saw Erika yesterday, out near the parkway," Vanessa said. "She had a big canvas bag, and she was picking up litter from the roadside. I stopped and offered to help, but she said it was something she had to do herself."

"I think she learned an important lesson from everything that happened," Frank said. "I hope so."

"Well, I learned something, too," Mike declared. "I still plan to be an investigative reporter, and this story will give me a great head start. But when it comes to detective work, the undisputed champions are Joe and Frank Hardy!"

Frank and Joe's next case:

There's a new brother team in town—Ed and Peter Mason—and they've got Frank and Joe's number. Ed's already put Joe down on the wrestling mat, and Peter's robots are sure to put Frank's science project to shame. And now the Masons are putting the moves on Callie and Vanessa. All's fair in love and war, but the Hardys don't even know what's at stake.

An even bigger test awaits them. Fenton Hardy has taken charge of a multimillion-dollar jewelry exhibit at the Bayport Museum, and his super-sophisticated security system has suddenly gone haywire. Realizing that much more than their reputations are on the line, Frank and Joe close ranks with their father in the fight of their lives with a criminal mastermind ... in *False Alarm,* Case #84 in The Hardy Boys Casefiles™.